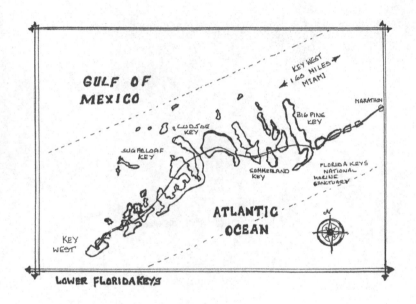

GULF OF
MEXICO

KEY WEST
160 MILES
MIAMI

MARATHON

CUDJOE
KEY

BIG PINE
KEY

SUGARLOAF
KEY

SUMMERLAND
KEY

FLORIDA KEYS
NATIONAL
MARINE
SANCTUARY

ATLANTIC
OCEAN

N

KEY
WEST

LOWER FLORIDA KEYS

RED, RIGHT, RETURN

June Keating Sherwin

iUniverse, Inc.
Bloomington

Red, Right, Return

iUniverse books may be ordered through booksellers or by contacting:

iUniverse
1663 Liberty Drive
Bloomington, IN 47403
www.iuniverse.com
1-800-Authors (1-800-288-4677)

Cover Art by Lindsay K. Sherwin

ISBN: 978-1-4620-5958-4 (sc)
ISBN: 978-1-4620-5959-1 (ebk)

Printed in the United States of America

iUniverse rev. date: 11/29/2011

For Lindsay, Case and Terry

1

MOST OF WRECKERS REEF sits under water. It can be dangerous for boaters since there's not a single marker to warn people off the low rocks. But if you're careful, the coral heads around the reef make it a perfect place to snorkel and fish. My family comes out here every time we visit the Florida Keys—but always in the big boat with Mom or Dad at the wheel.

Today was different.

Today was a test.

This was the first time my sister, Georgene, and I made the trip out to the reef all on our own. It's not far from the dock behind our house on Cudjoe Key, but we had to take the skiff outside the channel—out in the Atlantic Ocean—and then head south about a quarter mile off the coast of Sugarloaf Key. When we got to the reef, we climbed out and beached the boat up on the rocks.

"There're more clouds out there," Georgene quietly announced.

I lowered the camera and turned toward her. I'd been standing on the ledge of rock at the edge of the reef, staring through the lens at some men on an old boat. The longer I watched them work, the more I wondered, what were they hauling out of the ocean?

"Look, Chad," said Georgene. With the horizon behind her, she seemed taller than her official five foot six. Her high forehead and square jaw framed her straight, smallish nose, wide mouth, and expressive green eyes. My sister's eyes let you know exactly what she was thinking.

I'm five foot one right now. And bony, but I'm working on that with push-ups and extra laps in the practice pool. My hair used to be white-blond when I was little, but it gets darker and curlier every year. My slightly stubby nose will probably stay that way. As for my eyes, they're a mash-up of green and brown that people call hazel.

"Chad—" Worry lines creased Georgene's forehead as she pointed toward the horizon.

I could see the dark clouds. But I was more interested in what the men on the other boat were doing.

"They're way far away, Gene," I said, dismissing her warning. "Would you forget the clouds for a second? Look at that boat over there off Sugarloaf Key." I nodded at the boat across the water. "I think those guys are stealing something."

Georgene frowned. "What's that supposed to mean?"

"They might be taking lobsters out of somebody else's traps."

"If they are, it's certainly not our problem," she said, like that was the end of it.

I held out the little digital camera. "Here, look through the zoom lens."

Ignoring the camera, she slid her sunglasses on top of her head with a noisy sigh. "I see an old boat—I guess it's old," she speculated, peering across the water. "What makes you think they're stealing?"

She turned back to me, and I held her gaze. "The dive flag . . . there isn't one."

"*So?*" she snorted.

"It's more than that, Gene. That old fishing boat, or whatever it is, doesn't look like any of the other dive boats down here."

Her eyebrows angled up. That was good. Plus, I'd saved the best evidence for last. I pointed across the water, smiling, as I added, "*And*, they're bringing stuff up out of the water."

"Oooh, lock 'em up, officer! They look seriously suspicious." Clearly unconvinced, she elbowed me aside.

I suddenly remembered something. "Did you radio Dad while I was snorkeling?"

"No. I was reading." I frowned; we'd agreed before leaving the dock that we'd radio. She just sighed at me. "You can do it now, Chad. Radio's right there," she said, and she promptly switched on her music and sank back down on her towel.

"Didn't you say you'd do it?" I said, relishing her being in the hot seat.

Ever since her fourteenth birthday a few months ago, Georgene had changed. She used to be right there with me for every adventure. But now she was too busy being perfect.

I suppose her birthday wasn't the real reason she'd started acting differently.

She hadn't been the same ever since last summer, when Grandma Helen ended up in the hospital for emergency surgery. Mom took Georgene with her to help take care of Grandma Helen. Grandpa Jack needed help, too, since he has memory problems. I stayed home with Dad. After weeks of nursing Grandma back to her old self, Mom came home exhausted—but Georgene came home *good*.

After everything she did to help Mom with our grandparents, my sister discovered that she liked helping people.

Good for her.

But then she got it into her head that the best way to keep being helpful would be to fix everybody else's flaws—especially mine. She'd made it her personal mission to change *me*.

I had no intention of letting that happen.

I've always been curious. If something is interesting, I investigate. Georgene never had a problem with that before; but now, she's decided that my curiosity causes too much trouble. It's not my only flaw, according to her, but it's the one that most needs changing. I know sometimes my expeditions get us into tight spots, especially here at our vacation house in the Keys where there's so much to explore. But we've always managed to come out okay. I had to do some fast-talking to get the new Georgene to change her mind and come out to Wreckers Reef with me.

I missed the old Georgene.

I tapped her shoulder. "Gene?"

She plucked out an earpiece.

"Dad let us take the skiff out here to the reef—alone—only because we promised to radio him every half—"

"*You* promised, Chad. It's your trip," she cut in. "Eleven is old enough to phone home. You should have checked in by now."

I opened my mouth to let her know what I thought about that, but before I could get out a word, a fast-moving cloud moved in front of the sun, blocking it completely. The sky turned dark. In an instant, the clear, blue-green ocean became opaque and oily black. I couldn't see a foot down, much less the eighteen feet to the bottom where I'd just been snorkeling over huge coral heads. In the shadowy light, the reef's craggy rocks took on a strange grayish-yellow glow.

And then the wind picked up.

Gusting suddenly, it flung white foam off the cresting waves. Within seconds, goose bumps rippled along my arms. I grabbed a T-shirt out of the beach bag and Dad's expensive, new, marine GPS fell out onto the rocks. The little handheld receiver gets a signal from a satellite that can tell you where you are at any time. I'd brought it with me to test the coastal chart feature, but I'd wrapped it in my shirt earlier and then forgotten all about it.

"Look at those clouds, Chad!"

Forgetting the GPS for the second time that day, I turned away and pulled the shirt over my head. "Take it easy, Gene," I said. "It's just one cloud."

She pushed her sunglasses on top of her head and wrapped the bright orange beach towel around her. "It's not supposed to storm today," she said, eyeing the choppy waves.

"It'll blow over in a minute."

And in fact, a sliver of light appeared at the far edge of the cloud, growing bigger until the sun finally lit up the sky again, bright as before.

I stretched my arms out wide and soaked up the hot sun. The dazzling light blinded me after the darkness, but as my eyes adjusted to the glare, I caught the light glinting off the chrome fittings on the old boat across the water. I held up the camera and refocused on the men. Worries about storm clouds flew out of my head.

"Hey, Gene. That guy's still in the water over there. He's passing something heavy up to the other guy in the boat," I reported. "You need to see this."

I tapped the zoom button and brought the boat a little closer.

"Come look. He's climbing out," I continued. "Okay, now they're both hunched over the pile of stuff they brought up. One of the guys is scraping something off of one of—"

"We should probably head back, Chad," interrupted Georgene. But with a glance at the other boat, she dropped the towel on top of her bag and stepped over beside me.

I passed her the camera, and she propped it against her eye, muttering as she fiddled with the zoom. "I can't find the—*wait.* There it is. Okay, I see," she said. "Two guys on an old boat. They're moving stuff around over there. Is that what you're rattling on about?"

"That's exactly what I've been trying to tell you."

"They're loading those blocks, or rocks, whatever they are, into that big box on deck."

I shaded my eyes and stared, but I really couldn't see much without the zoom lens. "Let me have the camera," I said, pulling on her shoulder. Georgene shrugged me off and kept her eye on the lens. "I saw two guys, Gene. How many did you see?"

Just then, the wind shifted again. It blew with a two-toned whistling sound. I looked back over my shoulder and my heart skipped a beat.

Great blocks of steel-gray storm clouds were steering toward us. I turned and planted my feet wide on the sharp stones and watched the shifting clouds move across the sky. Gusting harder than before, the wind whipped over the island; it pushed the water higher on the rocks at the edge of the reef.

"I see two men. That's it, Chad," Georgene spoke up. She flipped the camera back to me and started packing her things in her bag. "Come on. We need to get moving."

"Okay," I said, adding quietly, "just one more quick look."

I turned to the boat across the water and held up the camera. The clouds were stacking up fast; it took only seconds for the towering thunderheads to completely block the sun. There was so little light, I could barely see the boat, much less make out what the men were doing on deck.

"*The skiff!*" cried Georgene, pointing to the edge of the reef.

2

I WADED OUT ONTO THE water-covered rocks but only got two steps before I stopped.

"No, no! It's going faster." I stared out helplessly at the skiff. The waves had lifted the little boat right off the rocks, and now it was drifting farther away with each gust of wind. The rising tide had covered the outer rim of the tiny island, leaving only about twenty feet of dry rock at the center.

"Come back, Chad. You can't catch it," Georgene said quietly.

I combed my fingers through my salt-stiffened hair and watched more clouds clumping up over the horizon. "They didn't predict any storms today," I said, shivering as the first drops of rain hit my shoulders.

"We've established that fact. But it doesn't matter what they predicted—it's here now." She'd shifted her beach bag to a patch of dry rock as she talked. Then she stuffed her towel into the bag and pulled out a rumpled tank top. She tugged the shirt on, pulling her long, tangled curls out of the way.

I went over and put my hand on her arm. "If you had radioed—"

"No, Chad," she grumbled. She pulled away and hooked her thumb at her beach bag. "We shouldn't have come out here at all. Just get the radio now and call Dad."

"We don't have the radio. It's on the boat."

"No—" She stared after the drifting skiff and sat down hard on the wet rocks. "I thought it was in my bag. We've got to get off of here before the tide comes up any more," she said in a small voice.

I dug her towel out of her bag and scrambled onto a rock jutting a foot above the rest of the reef. I gripped the sharp stones with my toes as I swirled the bright towel over my head like a matador's cape and hollered, "Hey! Help, help! Over here! *Hey!*"

Georgene eyed me over her shoulder. "They can't hear you." She backed away from the water lapping at her feet. "Besides, should you really call those guys over here?"

"What else can we do? See any buses out here? Marine Patrol boats?" My arms flopped down as I stepped off the rock. "The Marine Patrol always stops us when we dive for lobsters, but today, where are they?"

"There's no other boat out here."

"*Exactly*, Georgene, just . . . those guys over there." I gulped down a breath and let it out again, slowly, but my stomach wouldn't sit still. I squinted to make out what the men were doing on the other boat, but it was just a gray blur.

Georgene's hand came up. "*Listen*. Did they just start their engine?"

Cold rain pelted my back and shoulders as the faded gray boat swung slowly around and headed straight for us. Eyes ping-ponging north and south, I tracked both boats—theirs and ours. The little skiff pitched across the waves, away from us toward the open ocean, while the fishing boat plowed slowly toward us through the choppy waves.

3

THE OLD BOAT STRUGGLED closer, crawling up and over the rolling swells.

After about ten painfully slow minutes, it finally chugged up to shouting range of the reef. The old inboard engine spat black smoke. It roared and screeched as the man at the wheel throttled back and worked to keep the bow facing into the wind. Finally he cupped his hands and bellowed, "What're you kids doing out here?"

"Our boat!" I called, pointing toward the drifting dinghy.

"We'll get it," he yelled, without even a glance to see how far out it was. He flung a thumb at the stern and added, "Swim out and climb in—make it quick!"

I glanced at Georgene just as she shot me a sideways look. "Look at those guys," she said.

"I *am* looking."

I squinted as I tried to see the men's faces, but the boat was far enough away that I wasn't able to see much more than dark shapes. The man not piloting the vessel was bent over in the deep cockpit. I could only see the back of his head.

Another swell shoved the boat sideways. Georgene ducked down and wiped the blowing spray out of her eyes. "There's no way I'm getting on that boat," she declared, shaking her head.

I replied, "We have to do something." Paying no attention to the alarms clanging in my head, I grabbed her hand. "Come on!"

She yanked her arm away and sat back down.

"Come on, Gene. It'll be okay," I told her, deliberately ignoring the fact that I was trying to sell myself on the idea as much as her.

"No way," she said flatly. I knew I wouldn't get her to move again.

Without another word, I jumped into the water. I was hoping she'd follow me, but I didn't look back. The icy water felt nothing like the warm ocean I'd been snorkeling in earlier. Choppy waves splashed over my face as I swam an awkward sidestroke. Making big scissor kicks, I pulled my hands down through the water and tried to swim a straight line toward the old boat.

Halfway there, I stopped swimming and kicked big circles to keep my face above the waves as I looked around me. I could see Georgene still huddled at the edge of the reef, but her face was a blur.

I looked back at the boat. I could see the man in the cockpit now. The part of his face that wasn't covered with a dark beard was sunburned pinkish red. Turned sideways, with his hip braced against the side rail as he slung a line out to me, he completely blocked my view of the other man at the wheel. He was huge.

I kept kicking, but I didn't move any closer to the line floating on the waves a few yards away. Narrow slits stared out at me from under the brim of the big man's faded ball cap as he barked, "Grab that line. If that girlie's coming, she better haul it out here fast!" Then he arranged his mouth in a chilling smile and added, "That is, unless you plan on being shark snacks!"

He lashed the line to a cleat and reached below the gunwale. When he brought his hand up, he was pointing to the stern with a long metal gaff—a pole with a curved hook on the end used by deep-sea fishermen to lift big game fish out of the water by the gills. I couldn't see if he was aiming at a boarding ladder at the back of the boat, but I did notice that the gape of the hook on the gaff was huge—probably ten inches across—and as sharp as an ice-pick.

I suddenly had the feeling he didn't use it just for fish.

"Chad, *come back!*"

My legs ached. I couldn't hold my chin above the cresting waves much longer. Ignoring the ugly giant, I looked back at Georgene.

"See that?" she called excitedly. "Way down the shoreline?"

A spark of hope shot through me at the droning of the distant engine.

My choice was made. Although I had to fight the waves and current, I struggled back to the reef. I climbed up onto the rocks with the last of my strength and lay there, panting.

"That way." She pointed, and I lifted my head and looked across the water. "I think it's—"

Before she could finish, the fishing boat roared up to full throttle. It creaked and groaned as it crashed through the waves and slowly swung around the drowning island until I saw the name *Sand Dollar* painted in faded black letters across the transom. The big man in the cap stared at me; then he looked across the water to the boat headed our way. He yelled to the man at the wheel, but I couldn't hear the words. Bellowing thick smoke, the bow of the old boat came up out of the water and gradually leveled off as it picked up speed and headed back the way it came.

I got to my feet and hurried over to Georgene. Down the coast, I could just make out the flat hull of our Boston Whaler as it rode down a swell. "That's got to be Dad. Think he saw those guys?" The wind carried off my words as relief and anxiety tumbled in my mind.

We huddled together at the edge of the shrinking reef and watched the Whaler. "He's probably too far away to see those men. You'll have to tell him you were planning to get on their boat, Chad," she said.

"I had no choice, Gene. I was trying to get help."

Georgene nodded toward the old fishing boat, now running parallel to the shore. "They sure took off fast."

"I'm glad they're gone." I grabbed a towel and wrapped it around my shoulders. "There's no way I wanted to get on that boat," I admitted with a shudder.

"You sure seemed in a hurry a few minutes ago."

"That guy with the gaff was scary. Did you hear what he said?"

Her eyes narrowed. "No, not with the wind. What did he say?"

"He made a joke about us being shark snacks if we didn't get on their boat. But there was nothing funny about the way he said it. I didn't like the look on his face at all. I mean, could you see how big he was?"

"They were both scary as far as I'm concerned, Chad. You got me out here because you told me we'd just snorkel for a couple hours and then head home. And look what's happened!"

"We'd've been fine if this stupid storm hadn't blown in. Let's not tell Dad how creepy those guys were, okay?"

She glanced after the fishing boat. "Whatever we tell him, he's still going to be extremely upset. I can't believe we let ourselves get stranded out here. And lost the skiff . . ."

I'd only half-heard what she said as an image flashed through my mind. "Gene, listen, that stuff those guys hauled up? It wasn't just rocks or coral."

"What?"

"When I was watching them with the zoom lens, I didn't realize it then, but I saw shiny chunks in some of the rocks they were bringing up." I turned and listened as the rumbling grew louder.

"Dad's getting close," Georgene said, like she hadn't even heard me. "We need to get it straight, what we're going to tell him."

"Know what I think?" I said. "*Silver coins.* There were silver treasure coins in those rocks—that's what those shiny spots were where those guys had chipped at the rocks. I bet they dug them up from some shipwreck site. It's probably not a legal dive site, not for treasure anyway. And they were bringing stuff up—you know how strict the laws are to protect the live reefs."

"Chad, *enough.* I know about the reefs. Listen, Dad's—"

"Probably from a Spanish . . . uh, galleon. Those ships! You know, from hundreds of years ago?" I said. A slight shiver ran up my spine. "The ones that carried loads of treasure back to Spain? Remember? Those silver coins—the pieces-of-eight? With the markings on them for the king and stuff?"

Georgene suddenly looked interested again. "Like we saw at that treasure museum in Key West last year?"

"*Right.* Exactly. Those ships used to sail right past Florida—in big fleets for protection—especially when they carried expensive cargo like gold and silver coins. Some of them went down in huge hurricanes. Hey, I never thought of it before . . . I bet that's why they call these rocks Wreckers Reef. Ship wrecks, you know?"

"Treasure's not what we need to worry about right now," she offered. Angling for cover, she hunched behind my shoulder.

I craned my neck and looked back at her. "Bet you anything that was Spanish treasure those men were diving for," I insisted. "People still find stashes of silver and gold—jewels, too. Wreckers! That's what they used to call people who salvaged cargo after a storm. There're shipwrecks all over down here, buried under the sand."

"S-so?" Georgene sputtered through blue lips as she peeled a strand of wet hair off her mouth.

"Don't you want to know if that's what they found?" I asked. "I do."

Georgene stuck her chin over my shoulder. "Forget it, Chad. Dad's almost here."

4

"**H**OW DID YOU LET the skiff go? Didn't you see the clouds blowing in? You never radioed!" Back at the house, Dad's face puffed up like a blood-red blowfish as he fired questions at us.

I started to tell him about the men on the old fishing boat. I chose my words carefully; I was trying not to say too much.

"*You were going to get on their boat? Is that what you're telling me, Chad?*"

"The tide came up really fast. We had to get off the reef," I said weakly. The look on his face sucked the air right out of me.

"Hold it!" Dad held up his hand. "What about you, Georgene? What do you have to say about all this?"

"Things happened extremely fast," she said quietly.

"I thought you two could handle a trip on your own. I never expected such a nasty squall."

"Neither did we."

Georgene looked up. "Dad, those two men were—"

"*Fishing!*" I blurted, cutting her off before she could mention the blackened rocks. With the slightest nod, I signaled her to stay quiet about the treasure.

Her eyes lingered on mine for a moment. Then she turned back to Dad. "So, when the tide lifted the skiff off the reef, we were stuck out there. Those men came over to pick us up, but then—I guess when they heard your boat—they just took off."

"Did you have any idea who they were?" he asked.

"Never saw them before," I said.

I watched his left eyebrow arch higher as he stared first at me and then at Georgene without saying a word.

I asked my next question very quietly. "Are you going to call Mom?"

"Yes," he said, after thinking it over. "But she's taking Grandma to the doctor today. We'll all call her later."

Mom had gone straight to Stuart when the rest of us flew to Key West two days ago so she could help Grandma with some follow-up medical tests. She'd promised to get down here by the weekend. I'd been counting on it. But I wondered what she'd have to say about our latest adventure. The air whooshed out of my lips. Georgene just nodded.

Suddenly sounding much more upbeat, Dad announced, "So, Chad, I've got a plan. You and your sister will be staying out of trouble for at least the next two days. You two know that we count on rental income to maintain this house. Our realtor booked us a renter for the next few months—which is great news—but the place needs some major clean up first. Since Mom's busy with Grandma, I need you two to help me finish all the work that has to be done. Agreed?"

"Absolutely," I said.

Georgene smiled. "Agreed."

The next morning, over breakfast at the kitchen table, we divvied up the jobs on the list we'd made the night before. Once we all had jobs, Dad got started with painting the back bedroom while I headed out to the driveway to scour the big plastic trash buckets. I had to scrape off wads of brown gunk glued onto the plastic by months of steamy heat. Georgene swept and hosed out the carport.

After lunch, we moved to the backyard. Georgene and I hacked away at the tough vines growing across the stones. Working in silence, it took us nearly thirty minutes to bag the clippings; the gusty wind scattered leaves and vines everywhere.

Eventually Georgene, stooping to grab another pile of vines, asked, "Yesterday, when we told Dad what happened—why didn't you just tell him about the rocks?"

I set the bag down. "I didn't tell him because I didn't want him to stop us from going back out there."

Georgene's eyes widened. "*What?*"

"We have to find out if that stuff those men were bringing up really was treasure."

"Nobody's going back out there!" she snapped so fiercely it startled me. "We never should have gone in the first place. We got stranded because you were so busy spying on those men."

"Forget it, Georgene," I shot back. "Stop trying to pin it all on me."

And I am going back out there, I thought to myself.

I worked the rest of the afternoon without saying another word.

Dad made sloppy joes and french fries for dinner, favorites of mine; I gulped it all down way too fast. After dinner, I headed upstairs to shower. I took my time soaping up. Humming the first line of a reggae song I couldn't remember the words to, I thought about the crusted rocks. Just because they looked like black clumps didn't mean there wasn't treasure inside. I had to find out more. I let the hot water pound my sore shoulders; then I toweled off and headed to my room.

I only had an hour on the computer for my research before bed. Dad's orders.

The Wednesday clean-up was even worse. The boat shed had to be cleaned out, but first we had to empty it. Georgene and I didn't say a word for the whole hour it took to haul out all the stuff: trolling rods, spinning rods, all sorts of reels and lures, nets, chairs, life jackets, tackle boxes, loose tackle, buckets, masks, flip-flops, hammers, drills, screwdrivers, brooms, hats, sails, oars, fins, bikes and flags, every paint can and every last screwdriver. All of it got stacked up in the back breezeway.

I pushed the big broom and Georgene worked the smaller one as we swept out the shed. Every few minutes she'd shake her head and give me the *look*. I was pretty sure this one meant that I was the cause of all her problems. Nothing new there. I knew I couldn't change her mind about that, so I focused on the mess in the shed. Cobwebs drooped off everything. Palmetto bug droppings the size of BBs covered the cement floor under the storage cabinets, but the really disgusting part was the dead bugs.

Palmetto bug is just a nice name for extra-large cockroaches.

They're ugly brown bugs big as your finger, with long antennae that wave in the air. Worse than that, they have wings. When you're not looking, they can fly up and land right next to you. When I was really little, I was standing at the low toilet downstairs when a giant Palmetto bug landed on the rim. I didn't use that toilet again for years.

It was around eleven o'clock when all hell broke loose.

Without a word, Georgene had scooped up a mound of bugs into the shovel and tossed them at me. Clumps of dead bugs hit the side of my head, sticking in my hair, clinging to my grimy T-shirt.

"Georgene!" I howled as I spun across the breezeway, spraying cockroaches like confetti.

Georgene scooped up a new load. But before she could throw it, the broom I'd been holding whizzed past her head.

Dad suddenly appeared around the corner, paintbrush in hand. "Stop that, Chad!" he yelled.

"But *Dad*—"

The shovel clanged on the cement floor. "We were just having fun," Georgene hurried to explain.

"*Fun?* You chucked rotting Palmetto bugs all over me!" I yelped. The bugs crunched under my flip-flops as I danced around.

As he watched, Dad's angry expression looked more and more like a smile. "Enough," he said at last. "Believe it or not, you two are going to be brother and sister for a long time. Someday you're going to need each other. Trust me on that one."

I looked at Georgene. The expression on her face made it clear she didn't agree.

"All right. Back to work. Chad, you finish here. Georgene, get started on the front yard. Move it."

Georgene kicked aside the shovel and scooted around the corner of the house.

I, of course, was stuck with the bugs.

5

LATER THAT AFTERNOON, GEORGENE slunk around the corner of the breezeway. She was waving a white T-shirt on a stick like a peace flag.

"Hey. Truce, okay?" she grinned.

I knew better than to trust that grin. Without taking my eyes off her, I set the glass cleaner on the table in front of the sliding doors I'd just finished polishing. "What's your problem, Georgene?"

She shrugged. "I don't know. Maybe I wanted to shut you up for good about that stupid treasure. Sorry." She smiled. "But you were so hilarious with those bugs all over you!"

"Give it up, Georgene. You'd still be running if I dumped dead bugs all over you."

She shrugged again. Then she got still and said, "Listen—something's been bothering me. Do you think

Dad's okay with what we told him about that boat at the reef the other day?"

I wasn't sure I liked the direction the conversation was taking, but at least she'd stopped laughing at me. "I don't know. I guess he's been kind of quiet since we got back," I said. "Don't you think he's just worried about what could've happened?"

"Maybe. But I think you should tell him what you really thought about those men. If we tell him everything, maybe we can earn back some trust."

"I guess not telling something is pretty much the same as lying, isn't it?"

"You know it is."

"So what should we say?"

"Tell him what you told me," she suggested. "About how creepy you thought they were."

"Okay. I can do that. But, uh, don't talk about the treasure—not yet anyway, okay, Gene?"

"I thought we just agreed—"

By then, I was already down to the end of the breezeway and around the corner. I hurried through the carport with her calling after me, turned the corner at the front of the house, and took the stairs two at a time up to the kitchen.

An hour or so later, I watched from the bottom step outside as Dad's rusty old wood-paneled Grand Wagoneer crunched across the stones.

"Dad, can we talk?" Georgene blurted into his window, before he'd even shifted into park.

He nodded and turned off the engine. Then he grabbed his packages and the three of us trudged up the stairs.

I held the screen door open for Georgene and Dad and then followed them inside. Dad set the bags on the kitchen counter and sent us out to the screened porch to wait while he made a couple phone calls.

I sat there staring blankly at the books on the low shelf in the living room. Then I looked up at the phone chargers lined up on the little console table. The one on the end was empty.

My heart raced.

The empty charger was for Dad's brand-new marine GPS.

The one I'd left on the rocks out on the reef the other day.

I'd completely forgotten about it when the storm blew up. Apparently, so had Dad, but only because we'd been so busy, and he hadn't been fishing since then.

The racing in my heart became a dull pain. How could I tell him I'd lost his favorite new toy out at the reef—when I'd never asked him if I could take it in the first place?

The bedroom door swung open then. Dad walked out to the porch and sat down.

I couldn't even look at him.

Georgene started talking. "There's more we want to tell you about what happened the other day."

"Yes?" His eyebrows arched.

"Things happened pretty much the way we told you," I said, although I struggled to get the words out. I swallowed a couple of times. "But not . . . *exactly*. The people—the men on the boat . . . well, they were actually pretty scary-looking, and their boat was an old wreck."

"But they were going to help us out," Georgene added. "Help us get the skiff."

Dad hesitated before asking, "What scared you about them?"

Georgene looked at me.

"What else haven't you told me?" Dad demanded, suddenly sounding upset.

I could see we were headed for more yard work.

I tried to ignore the voice in my head. Should I tell him about the GPS? Georgene didn't even know I'd brought it out there. How could I tell him?

Focusing on the floor, I muttered, "Well, the skiff got loose. It was drifting away, and those guys were going to pick us up to take us out there to get the boat. . . ." The words trailed off.

"You know, you two," Dad said, his voice notching higher, "I couldn't care less about that boat. We were lucky the tide shifted before it drifted too far out, or we never would have picked it up. That boat's replaceable, but you two aren't. I never should have let—"

"But, Dad—" Georgene interrupted.

"Dad, we know what mistakes we made," I said at the same time. "Like we told you before, the storm just blew up so fast. You knew it wasn't supposed to storm that day."

He shook his head. "We're not talking about going to the movies here, Chad. Heading outside our bay to the reef, even if it is close to land and usually pretty routine, is just not a good idea."

"But we've been on boats down here for years," I replied.

Georgene added, "I've got my boater's Safety Ed card, too."

He raked his fingers through his hair with a frustrated sigh. "I know you're usually very responsible, Georgene. But it's not just you we're talking about here. Your little brother was out there too."

I could feel my ears glowing like a stoplight.

"Chad knows as much about boats and the water as I do—probably more," said Georgene.

I was shocked at what I'd heard: she was actually *defending* me.

"I can't have either of you taking off again. It's just too dangerous."

"What does that mean? We can't go back to the reef? Or we can't go anywhere?" Georgene cried.

Dad sighed again, but Georgene kept talking. "Going to the reef was Chad's idea. These *exploring* missions are always Chad's idea—"

The pain invaded my stomach now. The conversation had suddenly taken a wrong turn.

"And another thing—he's been tagging after me *everywhere* since he was two years old."

Whoa.

"I don't tag—"

Georgene's eyes dared me to make another sound. Turning back to Dad, she said, "Especially when we're here in the Keys, Chad's always following me, or he's off on some . . . *adventure.* Then I get dragged into it—and then I get blamed."

28

Under a fan on a screened porch, I suddenly felt like there was no air.

"Remember that time when we were here over spring break, back when Chad was really little, and he took off after me? When I walked around the corner to see Jeannie and Dennis's dog, Buddy, two blocks away? Chad thought I went down the other street, and he ended up inside the neighbor's house, and they couldn't hear you guys yelling for him? That wasn't my fault that time."

"I was three years old!" I sputtered. "Jeez! I haven't tagged after you or gotten you in trouble—"

"What about last spring?" she challenged back, jumping to her feet. "When you went out in the bay after that guy in the pontoon boat? You thought he was taking stuff out of Mr. Baxter's traps. Remember that? I got dragged into that one trying to help you out. And then I got grounded for two whole days because of you."

"Gene, I was just trying to—"

"He's always *investigating* something or other. It's got to stop."

"All right, Georgene. Sit down," Dad said. "We all know Chad's curiosity gets him into tight spots at times. But you're still supposed to look out for each other."

"I try. All the time, Dad," she said.

Unfortunately, I thought.

"But how am I supposed to get him to do what I say? Once he gets an idea in his head, there's no way I can stop him."

I know my sister thinks it's her job to keep me on the right path, but I had to wonder what it would be like if I'd shown up on the planet before her.

6

THE NEXT MORNING, EXCEPT for clumps of washed-up seaweed and palm fronds strewn around the yard, there was no sign of the storm that woke us during the night. After cringing in the dark with thunder booming over our heads, it was a relief to wake up to a beautiful day. The Whaler had made it through with only a snapped line and a couple dings on the hull. The bay sparkled under the blue sky, and even with the gusty breeze, the sun was warm.

Georgene and I took the flat-bottomed paddleboat and pedaled down the channel in front of the Baxter's house next door. I babied the clumsy rudder, jiggling it back and forth, so the light, plastic boat wouldn't turn in circles like a dog chasing after its tail. Slowly, we veered around the bend and headed down the canal behind the houses.

Years ago, people dredged deep canals on some of the larger islands. Cudjoe Key has several that cut across the island in a big grid. Waterways are like city streets here. Some people moor their boats behind their houses and use them to get around instead of cars.

On autopilot, Georgene and I steered the paddleboat right for our special spot. We'd been coming here to fish for years. Turning into the second canal, we pedaled up to the rusting VW Beetle hunkered on the bottom. There were schools of bright black-and-yellow snapper swimming in and out of the open windows. As I watched the fish, it occurred to me how much the car's rust-pitted, high-domed roof looked like the coral heads out at Wreckers Reef. A lot like them.

I hadn't said more than five words to Georgene since we left the dock. I was too busy thinking. The last couple days I'd been digging up details about treasure sites and local salvage companies. I already knew that people can't just go digging anywhere they think they'll find treasure. From a bunch of different websites, I also found out that treasure salvage is big business. Big business that's tightly controlled.

Salvage crews have to own the rights to dive the valuable old wrecks for treasure. They have to have special permits and licenses. They bring archeologists if the wreck is considered historic. And the sites can't be inside the marine sanctuary that protects the living coral reefs surrounding the Florida Keys.

I couldn't find anything recent about any sites off Sugarloaf Key. In fact, from what I'd found, there shouldn't be any treasure from Spanish galleon ship wrecks anywhere near Sugarloaf. But I learned that my suspicions were right; if they really did bring up treasure, no matter how it ended up here, they didn't do it legally. I had to check it out. I'd be doing something really important if I discovered that some ancient Spanish treasure was being stolen, or worse, that the reef was being damaged.

I shot a sideways glance at Georgene. She wasn't going to like what I had to say, but I needed to get her on my side if I wanted to get back out there.

"Gene?"

"Yeah?"

"What if those guys we saw the other day ... I mean, what if—"

"Not that again," she sighed. "Will you just give it up? Can't we just hang out today? The storm's over. We're okay. The boat's okay. Relax for once."

"But, Gene."

"No! Can't we—I mean, this is great, isn't it?" She flung her hands up toward the blue-glass sky. "We'll be back home, back in *school*, soon enough. Remember the freezing gray muck up there? Right now, we're here in Florida. We only have a few more days to be absolutely free. Please, *please*, just chill out and forget about your treasure fantasies, okay?"

"But that's what I'm talking about," I said. "This is no fantasy—it's real, and I have to do something about it. I just *know* those men were stealing something; there's no way that was a legal dive site. But no one will believe me. I have to get proof."

"So, what, you want to just take off after them? You want to be a treasure cop?" Georgene laughed. "Mom never should have taken you to that museum in Key West—you've been obsessed with shipwrecks and treasure ever since!"

"I wish Mom were here," I muttered.

Georgene stopped laughing. "I do too."

"I mean . . . Mom would get it. She'd want us to do something to protect the reef."

"Ha! Not if it meant tangling with those men again, and you know it, Chad. Just wait till she gets down here . . ." Her words trailed off. Then she narrowed her eyes and said, "Wait. Just what are you planning?"

"No one else saw those men out there—we did," I said. "No one's going to listen to us unless we get proof. We won't get anywhere near them. *Trust* me."

"*We?* Don't put me in your stupid plan," Georgene cried, shrinking away from me. "'Forget about it, Chad. I have no intention of getting anywhere near those guys ever again."

I grabbed the steering handle as the boat rocked back and forth. "Relax, Genie." I grinned. "I told you—we're not going anywhere near them."

"You're nuts!" Georgene swiped her hand through the water and splashed my face.

I ducked and scooped watery gunk off the floor of the paddleboat and flung it at her. Speckled green slime oozed down her forehead. Georgene sputtered and spat out the greasy stuff.

"Fine. It's *on*."

I reached for more ammunition, but Georgene slammed me with her shoulder first. I barreled over the side, head first. Before I figured out which way was up, I'd gulped a mouthful of water. I kicked to the surface and came up thrashing.

"Ha! Gotcha!" Georgene grinned. She leaned over the side and stuck out her hand.

After dinner I stood at the edge of the dock, casting a light rod out into the still bay as the sun hung on the horizon. I'd thought that going fishing would help me forget about Dad's GPS, but instead it was all I could think about—that, and the treasure at the reef. I'd decided to tell Dad I'd lost his new GPS. I just hadn't decided how.

Georgene's wooden Dr. Scholl's sandals clomped across the boards.

"Shhh!" I hissed. "You're scaring off the fish."

"Chad, Dad wants you up at the house."

I reeled in my line. "We'll have to go soon—back out to the reef, I mean—to find out what those men were up to."

"Dad wants—" She eyed me for a few seconds. Then she asked, "What makes you so sure those guys will come back?"

"They have to come back. Up until today, the weather's been lousy. Blowing every day since we got stuck out there, right?"

"Yes, but—"

"They found stuff the other day, coins and stuff," I explained, as I picked up a small plastic bag of hooks and dropped it into the tackle box. "They definitely weren't finished hauling it all up when we called for help after the weather got nasty. Right? So they have to go back and finish what they were doing. And with the calm weather today, the water out there tomorrow should be nice and clear again." I snapped the lid closed and stood up.

With a self-satisfied smirk, Georgene poked me in the arm. "Perfect. That's a great idea, Indiana, but there is no way on earth I'm going back out there with you. And you're not going anywhere either. That's what I came out here to tell you. Dad's got an all-day meeting for work in Key West. He made plans for you to go next door and help Mr. Baxter finish a project, and then you can help him rig some new rods too."

"Where are you going?"

"Nowhere. Jeannie—remember Mom's friend with the golden retriever? Well, she finally got a day off from her job at the clinic, so she's coming over here to paint fish T-shirts. I promised to teach her way back in the summer, but we never had the chance before. I'm taking them home for my friends at school."

7

EARLY THE NEXT MORNING, Mr. Baxter and I were down in his workshop organizing tools on a new shelf system, when Mrs. Baxter came down to tell me that Georgene and Jeannie were going up to Big Pine to pick up some more painting supplies.

As soon as Jeannie's car had pulled out of the driveway, I told the Baxters that I needed to go back to the house and check my e-mail for my swim team schedule and confirm with my coach back home. It was the best excuse I could think of. I waited until Mr. B was back in his workshop before I headed over to our house.

I grabbed some gear and hurried down to the dock; then I jumped into the skiff and pushed off before I could change my mind.

I swung the boat around the plastic pipe in front of our house and headed across the shallows, chanting,

"Brown, brown, you're aground," as I weaved around the rocks and brown spots that littered the bottom like land mines. The last thing I needed right now was a bashed hull or getting stuck out here in the sand.

As the water got deeper and turned army green, I inhaled the fresh salt air, glad to be out in safer water. Banking to the west, I picked up speed and bent my knees as the skiff bumped over the small chop. The boat headed straight across the middle of the wide bay.

At the western end, I passed a group of wooden boats anchored in the shallows where there were no houses. I steered just a little closer. Natural sea sponges covered the deck of the large wooden fishing boat. Four shallow boats the size of skiffs bobbed behind it. They were probably bright a long time ago, but now the boats had coats of faded and peeling paint. As I watched, several men in wide-brimmed straw hats slung bamboo poles over their shoulders and clambered out of the lead boat and down into the smaller boats.

I motored along, watching the boats spread out across the shallows as the men worked the long poles. They stared into the shallow water, gently poling and gliding along. Every few moments one of the men jabbed his bamboo pole into the sand, brought up a dripping sea sponge, and dropped it into his skiff.

Just then, the lead boat swung sideways with the current. I studied the low, boxy pilothouse. It looked familiar.

In fact, the whole boat looked familiar.

I focused on the open cockpit and the hairs on the back of my neck pricked up. The old fishing boat from the other day! It had the same weathered boards and blocky lines.

Didn't it?

And then I spotted a wooden bin behind the pilot station that looked a lot like the box we'd seen on the other fishing boat. I scanned the stern, thinking I might see *Sand Dollar* lettered there, but the transom was completely covered with fishing nets.

I couldn't see much of the men's faces on the sponge boat. Not with the big straw hats. I turned away, wondering if I was just imagining things. Georgene always said I did.

But still.

Were these sponge fishermen connected somehow to the men from the other day? I bumped up the throttle and kept my eyes on the water in front of me.

Minutes later, when I got to the main channel, I swung the wheel north and started past the small sailboats anchored off the beach at the KOA campground. Then I cut to the right and steered between the boats moored at the cement bulkheads lining the canal. Puttering along, I put the sponge fishermen out of my mind and focused on my plan. The web had good information, and I'd even checked Mom's books on Spanish treasure, but I needed lots more answers if I was going to find out what those men had been up to out at the reef.

That's why I was headed over to talk to Turner Stiles, the high school guy who worked the pumps at the marina on the backside of Cudjoe. Maybe Turner could help me find what I needed. Then I had to get back to the house before Georgene got home, and definitely before Dad. I'd had more than enough cockroach cleaning for one week.

8

I SLID UP TO THE bulkhead at the marina and climbed the ladder. After tying the skiff to the closest cleat, I hurried inside the small store beside the docks.

I grabbed a lemon Gatorade and a package of Slim Jims and plunked my money on the counter. "Is Turner here today?" I asked, staring up at the man there. This wasn't the usual guy, the owner, Harry. A scraggly, gray-speckled beard hid the lower half of the man's face. Creases in the blotchy pink skin around his eyes deepened as his whiskers parted in a slow smile. I tore open the Slim Jims and chomped down, focusing on chewing the tough meat to avoid his curious stare.

"Out back, restocking bait coolers," he drawled, and angled his head toward the back wall. "Whadd'ya need?"

He was probably just trying to be helpful, but I wasn't talking to anybody but Turner.

"I'll just head out back and find him. Thanks, mister." I could feel the man's pale eyes on the back of my head, but I kept moving out the screen door.

I found Turner around back, scooping live shrimp into circulating bait wells.

"Hey, Turner," I called.

Dad and I had met Turner when we gassed up the Whaler one day last spring. He had to be sixteen by now. I knew he lived with his uncle in a double-wide, pre-fab house built up on pilings over on the back side of Cudjoe, but I'd never been over there.

Last time I'd seen him, I was casting for baitfish out on the bay. I couldn't get the net to spread out in a big circle before it hit the water, which is the only way to get the fish in the net. Turner happened to be cruising past and stopped to help me. Once he showed me what I was doing wrong, it only took two tries for me to throw a perfect circle. I needed lots of baitfish since Dad and I were going out to do some bottom-fishing off the old shipwreck the next day. Turner ended up coming out with us. It was a fantastic day; we caught enough fish for dinner for us and sold the rest of the fish to the market over on the highway.

Turner lifted his head and pushed away from the cooler. His long frame unfolded until I had to tilt my head back to see his face; he was that much taller than I remembered.

"Hey, Chad. It's been a while. What's up, man?" he said with a friendly grin, brushing a clump of brown hair out of his intensely blue eyes.

A while back, Turner had told me his uncle worked part time for a treasure salvage crew out of Key West. I don't know why I didn't think of it before, but Turner might just be able to tell me something about the site over on Sugarloaf.

"Well, I need to ask you something," I started.

"Shoot."

"Uh, have you ever heard anything about a dive site off Sugarloaf Key—way down on the south side of the island? From your uncle, maybe? Uh, I mean like one of those old time ship wrecks—a dive site where there would be treasure—gold or silver coins—that kind of stuff?"

Turner set the bait scoop on top of the cooler and squinted down at me. "Who wants to know?"

"Me, that is, I do," I answered, wondering why he'd suddenly stopped smiling.

"Whaddya need to know something like that for?"

"Can you just tell me? It's . . . important."

He kept staring at me and shoved his hands in the pockets of his jeans. "Well, maybe. I just might know something like that. But if I do, it's not for anybody else's information. You're okay, Chad, but this has to stay between you and me." He rocked up and down on his heels.

I nodded and swallowed. "Got it. Right. Exactly. Just for me. No problem," I babbled.

"Well . . . I saw this chart one time, maybe a couple years back. I probably wasn't supposed to see it, but my uncle left it on the kitchen table and I looked it over before he put it away. Anyway, it was all marked up. I remember it because of the symbols somebody had used—figure eights, you know, like the number eight? And those silver coins from Spanish ships are called pieces of eight. So the chart showed a couple spots over on the ocean side of Sugarloaf. In close. Had the GPS coordinates too, for radar finders, like. But I don't remember those."

"Whose chart was it? Think you could find it?"

"No, probably not. After that one time, Uncle Skip never brought any charts back to the house any more. At least, not that I ever saw. So what's up? What're you trying to find?"

I suddenly wasn't sure I was ready to tell Turner what I suspected. I didn't know if he really was the kind of guy who could help another guy out and keep his mouth shut. I had no idea if I should trust him, or what he'd do if he found out about the treasure site.

If that's really what it was.

I dug at the dirt with my toe. Then I glanced at my watch and saw it was already ten fifteen.

I started to talk.

9

AHALF HOUR LATER, I tied off the skiff at the dock behind our house. Turner swung by and picked me up in his boat, and then we headed over to his house to check out his uncle's old boat shed.

Unfortunately, a quick search turned up no chart—or anything else, for that matter. Turner stood in the center of the small room, turning slowly as he looked over the cabinets and shelves we'd just searched. "Mmmm . . . maybe we should check the dive boat. He could have some charts stashed there. I really don't know, Chad."

"Let's go," I said, already moving toward the door.

"What's your plan if we find the charts?"

"I don't really have a plan yet. But if we find the charts, and they show old treasure sites . . . then maybe I can find proof what those men were bringing up out there."

"Looters at a protected reef? Probably not something you want to tackle on your own."

"But I need to find some sort of proof before I tell anyone about this."

"Let's just see if we find any charts first."

Turner and I hurried back down to the dock and jumped into the boat. His uncle kept his dive boat way over on the other side of Cudjoe, in the canal behind the bait shop on highway A1A.

Minutes later, we coasted up to the bulkhead and tied off. Turner checked the pilot station while I dug through the storage bins along the gunwales.

"Any luck?" I looked up hopefully, a few minutes later.

"Nope."

I rushed down the steep companion ladder and landed on the deck in the lower cabin. I stood there scratching my head as I looked around the small space.

Still up on deck, Turner stuck his face into the doorway. "Why don't you check those shelves back there under the bunks?" He pointed to a couple low shelves built into the sides of the V-berth in the bow of the boat.

I worked my way forward, stepping over bins and loose dive gear strewn around the deck. Inside the cramped cabin, I crouched down and searched through the gear on the shelves. No charts.

I headed back to the small cabin and dug around in the plastic bins packed with every kind of fishing gear and dive supplies. It took several minutes, but I finally finished looking through all the gear.

Still no charts.

Suddenly, a powerful outboard engine rumbled nearby. I listened and realized it had to be right alongside. I began heading for the stairs when a deep voice commanded, "Young man, hold it right there." I froze in my tracks and didn't move. It took me a second to realize they were talking to Turner up on deck.

Rushing up the steps, I came face to face with a deeply tanned man in uniform—a Marine Patrol officer. He must have just boarded the boat.

"Hi there, Officer," Turner greeted him anxiously.

"What business do you two have on this boat?" the man demanded, looking around at the mess of charts and gear strewn across the deck.

Turner explained. "Oh, you see, Officer, we're trying to find a special trolling rig my uncle keeps on board."

"Your uncle?" I couldn't see his eyes behind his mirrored aviators, but his voice didn't sound very friendly.

"Yes," Turner nodded, "this is my uncle's boat. He sent me here to find the fishing lure."

"Is that right?" said the officer, still scanning the deck. He ducked down and peered into the cabin below. "I suggest you get him on the radio right now."

"He's out with a dive party," Turner said, glancing at me.

I looked down at the deck and stayed silent. This was Turner's show.

"We're checking along the wharf here every day now. There's been a number of burglaries on boats this past month."

Turner reached into his pocket and pulled out his wallet. He dug out a rumpled business card his uncle had given him and handed it to the officer.

"All right. I'll take this for now. We'll be checking in with your uncle, though."

Turner nodded. "Sure."

"Officer?" He turned to look at me. "Some men are fishing sponges out of the shallows down at the west end of Cudjoe Bay. Is that legal?"

Shaking his head, he said, "You two ought to focus on your own business right about now, don't you think?"

I nodded, but added, "Yes, but can they do that?"

He hopped back aboard the cruiser. "I'm gonna check on you two—don't think I won't."

A second officer spoke up as he pushed off, "And son, you should know, those boats are legal for sponging if they're licensed and they take only mature sponges."

The other man tapped the throttle and called back, "Let's not find you visiting any more of these boats now, you hear? You two jokers may not get so lucky the next time."

I stood still for a minute listening to Turner mutter, "This was not a good idea. Jeez. Wait till Uncle Skip finds out. He's not gonna like hearing from the Marine Patrol. And he's definitely not going to be happy to hear we were digging through his stuff."

"I know," I said, happy to be free of the officers. But I wasn't giving up. I rushed back down the stairs and started back across the cluttered cabin.

Turner stood at the top of the ladder, looking down at me with a frown. "We gotta clear out of here, Chad."

I stopped digging and started to head back up to deck. Then it hit me; I knew where they were. I kicked a big bin aside and found a small compartment down low on the outer bulkhead that I'd missed before.

Score.

"Turner!" I called excitedly. "There's charts in here! Piles and piles of charts."

Turner hit the deck with a thud. He ducked down and rushed over to help me clear the gear off the small table so we could look at the charts. At first, they were just charts for the waters off the Florida mainland, the east coast, Vero Beach, and Sebastian; and lots more charts for west coast areas like Boca Grande and Fort Meyers. But there at the bottom of the pile we found three more heavily used charts. These charts were for the lower and middle Florida Keys.

Sugarloaf Key, to be exact.

10

THE WATER WAS PRACTICALLY flat. Turner cut the engine, and I dropped the anchor, watching it sink through the clear green water until it hit the sandy bottom. We were off the coast of Sugarloaf, a little east of where the old fishing boat had been anchored the other day.

My idea was to check out the spot we'd found on the chart—it seemed to be the same location off Sugarloaf where the men had been diving the other day—and see if there was anything down there. Turner laughed when I told him about losing Dad's new GPS, but he agreed that after we checked out the dive site, we could stop at Wreckers Reef to look for the GPS before we headed back to the house.

I pulled on my fins, grabbed my snorkel, and followed Turner over the side.

"Do you think this is it?" I asked, treading water easily with the huge fins on my feet.

"Best I can tell," he said. "It's probably seventeen feet deep here. So, I can give you my weight belt. You can't weigh more than what? Ninety, ninety-five pounds?"

"Yep. Something like that."

"I'll take some weight off," he said, removing a couple of the small weights on the rubber belt before he handed it to me.

I adjusted the belt around my waist. "I didn't even think about a weight belt when I grabbed my gear. I was just in such a rush."

"We should have brought air tanks, really. Are you certified so you can dive with scuba gear?"

"Not yet," I admitted, "but I know the technical stuff. I've read everything. And I've done shallow free-diving down here with my folks. I'm taking the test on my birthday at the end of the summer."

"That's cool. Doesn't matter, anyway. Like I said before, I don't have much more time today. We can check this spot out real quick, but then I gotta get back."

"Wreckers Reef first, right?"

Turner grinned. "You are one interesting little dude, my friend," he said. Then, sticking the snorkel in his mouth, he dove. I watched his fins slip below the water.

I spat in my mask and rinsed it with salt water. With a deep breath, I pulled it on, adjusting it so it sealed tight to my face. I stuck the snorkel in my mouth, blew the water out of the tube, and dove down after Turner.

I kept the fingers of one hand pressed against the nose pocket on my mask and blew out to release the pressure in my ears. I worked the big fins in small flutter kicks. Finally I got down to the bottom. I kept to the open area away from the long coral reef as I swam over the rippled sand. It was so quiet. The bottom almost looked brown in the dark green light.

After a few seconds, I kicked back up for air. Turner surfaced right after me.

He pulled off his mask and took a deep breath. "Did you see that?"

"See what?"

"Behind the reef. There's a big hole back there."

"A drop off, you mean?"

"No . . . not like normal. It looked like the sand had been moved."

"Show me?" I asked.

"Over here," Turner said. He swam about six yards and then dove on the other side of the reef I'd just been skirting. I followed.

Like a dolphin, moving his whole body in a smooth rippling motion, he cut through the water very quickly. I had to flutter-kick furiously to keep up with him. I heard Turner grunting into his snorkel as he tried to tell me something. But I couldn't understand. He pointed at a shadowy ledge in front of us.

I was out of air again. I left him and swam up, spitting out my snorkel after I surfaced. I was coughing hard to get rid of the huge gulp of water I'd swallowed, when I saw my sister staring down at me.

11

"**Y**OU ARE TOAST, LITTLE brother!" Georgene snapped.

Her eyes dared me to challenge her, but she didn't need to threaten me; I had no energy to argue. I pulled myself up into the skiff and lay there panting, hoping she would keep it under control when Turner came up.

Just then, he swam over. Hanging on the side of the skiff, he smiled at Georgene and said, "How's it goin', Gene? How'd you find us out here?"

She gave him a little wave but didn't say anything.

Turner looked at me. "Chad, did you see it? There's a big hole down there right beside the reef."

"I just saw a dark patch when you were yelling into your snorkel. I had to come up for air."

"I was trying to tell you to look down. Something moved a bunch of sand. Not like it just shifted from a storm or something. There's a rubble pile down there, too. Blocky encrusted stuff. I didn't get a very good look."

"I want to see. I'm going back down—"

"No you are not!" Georgene said. "Listen to me; you're not going anywhere. Except home. I can't believe you left the Baxters' and came back out here."

"Did you hear what Turner just said? There's something down there. I told you there was."

"That's not your problem. Your problem is getting home *right now.*"

"Georgene—"

"It's a good thing Jeannie and I didn't go all the way to Big Pine like we planned. When we got home, Mr. Baxter was at our house, looking for you. He said you gave him some story about an e-mail when you left him in his workshop—what was that about?"

"I had to go see Turner. Mr. Baxter never would have let me go if I told him that. How'd you figure out where I went?"

"I looked around the house for you, but then I saw the skiff had moved. I found a Slim Jim wrapper on the deck. You always get those at the marina—and you always leave your trash in the skiff—so I called over there; they said Turner had left about a little over an hour earlier. That's when I knew where you went."

"Gene—"

"I know you're treasure-crazed, Chad, but I really can't believe you came back out here. Even with Turner," she said, glancing at him. "The only reason I came after you was to make sure you got home right away. There's no way I'm going to let you spoil the rest of this trip for Dad, or me. And especially Mom. She's missed most of it."

Turner let go of the gunwale and dropped back into the water with a splash. "Okay, well. Catch you later, Chad—and, uh, you too, Georgene," he said, with a little smile. "You gotta keep it quiet about that chart we found today, okay, kiddo? That's key, or I'll get torched by my uncle. Anyway, it's been . . . interesting. Good luck with the search." With a little wave he swam back to his boat, hauled anchor, and disappeared.

"Listen to me, Gene. We found a chart! It was on Turner's uncle's boat. It's for Sugarloaf Key and it shows marks for treasure *right* where we were diving."

"Chad—"

"You heard what Turner saw. We have to do something about it."

"Not right now, we don't," she said.

"Okay. We'll figure out something when we get home. I'll talk to Turner. But we need to make a quick stop at Wreckers Reef."

Georgene let out an exasperated sigh. "Why in the world would we go there now?"

"I need to see if Dad's GPS is still there."

"And why would Dad's GPS be out there?"

"I took it out with me the other day. It fell out on the rocks when I put my shirt on . . . then the storm blew in, and I just forgot about it."

"Dad's *brand-new* GPS?" Her voice had gotten very shrill.

I cringed and nodded.

"You've got to be kidding, Chad. There's no way that thing is still there. If it is, it has to be worthless by now."

"You don't know that. It's waterproof. It's meant for boats. I have to at least check and see. If I find it, that's one less thing for Dad to be upset with me about."

"Chad—"

"Look, you chased Turner off. He was going to take me. I don't care what you say—I'm going over there right now."

"You are *unbelievable*. Do you have any idea what a world of trouble you cause, little brother?"

"Stop calling me that."

"Someday I'm going to make you pay for this. You've got five minutes. Let's go."

When we got to the reef, we tied the bowline to one of the big rocks. After a long drink from Georgene's water bottle, I worked my way across the rocks while Georgene went over to the higher rocks and looked around.

I bent down and walked slowly, so I could see into the dark crevices. Near the edge of the reef, I caught a glimpse of something blue. I stuck my hand down between the rocks and pulled out the blue woven lanyard attached to the GPS.

"I found it!" I yelled, barely believing it even though I held it in my hand. I tapped the power switch, but the unit didn't light up.

I stood up and stuck the GPS in the pocket of my board shorts and sealed the Velcro flap as I walked over to Georgene. She stood at the edge of the reef, staring across the water. She glanced over at me and then pointed toward Sugarloaf's low, overgrown coastline.

"See that little cut? By the clump of palm trees?" she said, quietly.

I looked where she was pointing, but all I could see was a wall of mangroves.

"Over there. Farther down." She motioned toward the shoreline.

It was a boat. A blocky boat cutting through an opening in the trees.

"Is that the same boat?"

"Just a sec. The big binoculars are in my beach bag." She grabbed them and aimed them at the boat.

"Is it those guys?"

"Looks like them."

"Can I see?"

"No. We're out of here." Georgene wheeled around and started toward the skiff.

I took the binoculars out of her hand as she hurried past me. "Wait just a sec so I can focus . . . Hey! It *is* the same two guys."

She looked back at me. "Come on. Now!"

"Same spot as the other day." My stomach tightened. "I knew it—just like I told you yesterday. I knew they had to come back!"

"You won't be so cocky when Dad finds out what you've been up to," Georgene fired back. She turned back to the skiff. "Let's get going, Chad. I'm not running into those two again."

"Easy, Georgene. They're way over there. And besides, they're too busy to notice us." She took the bowline off the rock and pulled the skiff in close to the reef, and then dropped her bag on the deck. With the bowline in her hand she stood there, peering across the water.

I turned the dial and brought the men into focus. "Turner's chart was right, Gene. See that machine on the deck? I bet that's some sort of lift—to bring up the heavy stuff, you know?"

I felt torn between getting out of there and finding out exactly what those guys were doing.

"It looks like the big one has something heavy. Okay, there he goes again. He dove under."

"What's he bringing up?"

"Looks like that big crank thing with the cable—what's it called, a winch—they're using that to haul those blocks up. He dropped the hook again. Now they're raising the stuff out of the water."

"Can you see what it is?"

"No. Can't tell. There's a net around a blocky thing. They're hauling it over the side, see? I bet you anything that's silver treasure. We should take a picture." I glanced at the beach bag in the skiff. "Did you bring the camera? You keep everything in that bag of yours, usually."

Georgene's eyes bugged out. "Absolutely not! We are not taking any pictures. We're not even supposed to be out here. What was I thinking? Oh, right—I had to come after my disturbed brother—that's what I was thinking."

I climbed in over the stern.

"We're not going close. We just need to get the sun behind us and the zoom will take care of the rest. Trust me, they're busy—they'll never even notice us."

I saw her shoulders slump a little. "One shot—*that's it*," she snapped. "Then we're going."

I revved the handheld throttle and the small boat jerked forward.

12

I WAS RIGHT: THE MEN on the other boat didn't even notice us.

Well, not until I slowed the skiff so Georgene could take the picture.

I backed off on the gas, letting the engine idle while she fiddled with the zoom lens. But as I let it off a little more, the engine suddenly sputtered. I twisted the throttle to give it just a little gas.

No response.

I gunned it again, but the engine wouldn't even hiccup. I realized then that we were drifting away from the reef. I wiped the sweat off my forehead and pumped the little black bulb on the fuel line. I hit the throttle again.

Nothing.

I forced the lump back down my throat as I realized the current was pulling us toward the old fishing boat.

"Georgene?"

She lowered the camera, followed my eyes, and carefully moved back beside me.

"It won't start, Gene. I tried everything," I whispered, shifting over to the middle bench.

"Here, let me try." She took hold of the throttle and twisted it downward. The engine coughed and whined before it screeched once and died out.

Now less than three hundred yards away, the men stood at the fishing boat's rail. They were staring in our direction.

Georgene cranked the starter again. She pumped the gas line and then went back to the throttle. This time the engine didn't even wheeze.

I dug the small hand-held radio out of her bag. Flipping the switch and putting the radio up to my ear, dimly wondering why it didn't crackle or even hum, I spoke into the receiver, "*Fin Again, Fin Again*, this is *Small Stuff*, come back?"

I looked across the water, hoping to spot Turner in the distance, but I knew he was long gone.

I pressed the talk button and tried again, but the radio let out a squawk and then went silent.

"Didn't this thing get charged?"

Georgene grabbed her cell phone and held it up, turning in a slow circle as she squinted at the small screen. I knew she was looking for a signal. I also knew she wasn't going to get any bars out here—she knew it, too, but she didn't seem to want to acknowledge that just now.

The other boat was moving now. It cruised closer, and all we could do was watch.

"We'll tell them we're out here fishing. It'll be okay, Gene."

"Chad, I think we—"

"We'll be okay, Gene."

Georgene pumped the throttle one more time as she watched the men coming closer.

As the boat approached I saw the winch I'd spied earlier. The boat swung a wide turn and I looked over the length of it at the waterline. I realized it was smaller than I'd estimated. At about twenty yards away, the driver throttled down, and they coasted up to us. I hung on to the sides as the skiff bobbed over the wake from the other boat.

The big man from the other day reached over the side with a boat hook and snagged our bowline. He towed the skiff around to the boarding ladder at the stern of the fishing boat and grabbed hold of the bow.

"Made it off that rock, did you?" he said, with that same awful smile. A fat, bluish vein pulsed on his reddened forehead.

"Yeah, our dad came and got us." I glanced back at Georgene in the stern. She was leaning as far away from him as she could get in the tiny boat.

"But you're back out here today?"

I grabbed an old bait bucket off the deck and held it up. "Been fishing. Didn't do so hot; we had a snapper on a little while ago, but it got away."

His expression didn't change. "Is that right? Funny, you two are out here again on your own," he said, shifting his eyes from me to the man at the wheel. "We sure didn't expect to see that."

The driver muttered, "That's enough, Vic. Let's get a move on." He slid the throttle into gear.

Vic still had hold of the skiff; it rocked over a little wave, and I felt something hit my foot. I glanced down, and tried to nudge it back under the bench with my toes, but we rocked again and my toes slipped off the camera. It slid back out in full view, the telephoto lens fully extended.

"You two are finished sightseeing for today," he snapped. "Gimme that camera!"

"Leave us alone!" cried Georgene.

I grabbed the paddle and pushed it against the other boat as hard as I could. Georgene lunged across the skiff and pushed with me, but the man kicked the paddle away, and we both fell back down in the skiff.

Leaning over the side, he was barely two feet away when he shouted, "Play time is over. I want that camera!"

"You have no right—"

He yanked the skiff closer, cutting me off, and stuck his face up to mine. "Give it," he demanded.

"Take it. Leave us alone." Georgene held the camera out. He snatched the camera and flung it far across the rolling swells.

"You got the camera. We're going," I said, hoping my voice wasn't as squeaky as it sounded to me.

Still holding the skiff, the big man turned to the other man at the wheel. "So what do we do now, Blicker?"

"These two got lucky the other day. But now we've got to shut them up. No telling what they saw, or who they squawked about us to," he replied.

Busy watching Blicker, I didn't even see Vic reach down and grab my wrist. Without a word, he hauled me up the little ladder, over the rail, and onto the deck of the old boat. Then he dragged Georgene out of the skiff and plunked her down beside me. He quickly lashed the line to a cleat to tow the skiff behind the bigger boat.

Georgene scooted closer. I felt her shaking as her shoulder pressed against mine.

"Don't move," barked Blicker. He quickly tied my wrists and then Georgene's with the rough rope of a mooring line.

"You can't do this!" I cried out.

"Shut it—*now!*" Vic commanded.

"Let us go!" Georgene yelled. She sounded very scared.

"Quiet, both of you. Get down and stay there," ordered Vic as he shoved me below the gunwale. Already low, curled against the side, Georgene leaned over to me.

"We have to do something," she whispered. Her huge eyes darted from me to the men and back again.

I pressed against her shoulder, breathing hard, and tried to think of something—anything—to help us escape.

"Gotta take these two to Purcell. He'll decide what to do with them," Blicker muttered, as he turned back to the wheel. As the two men talked, I looked around the old boat.

I stared at the blackish blocks in the storage well. They did look like rocks at first, but then I saw the sun glint off a patch of shiny metal buried in the dark, rough-edged coating. A couple loose silver coins lay just inside the locker next to two blackish rectangular bars. Another block—this one with lots more shiny coins—stuck out behind an old toolbox.

I glanced at Georgene just as she looked up at me. I nodded at the storage well. Georgene turned to look, but quickly dropped her head again as the men started talking.

Vic looked over. I lowered my head, locking eyes with Georgene.

"Forget those kids, Vic," Blicker said, as he swung the boat around. "What you ought'a care about is gettin' this stuff to Purcell. He won't take it lightly if we don't show by three, right?"

He gunned the engines and brought the boat up on plane, and it skimmed over the glassy water.

13

WE RAN SOUTH FOR a good fifteen minutes. I watched the water without spotting another boat the whole time. As we sat there, helpless, I whispered to Georgene that maybe we should try to jump overboard. She shook her head, lifting her bound hands just an inch. I knew she was letting me know that we'd never make it to shore with our hands tied like that.

Soon Blicker swung in close to the coast, steering through the reefs and tiny islands. Slowly, we tracked a narrow stream of water that cut through the shoreline for almost a quarter of a mile before opening out into a wide, protected bay. The shallow water was blotched with grassy shadows.

It's not deep enough, I thought. *We'll never make it.*

Vic stood watch at the bow, signaling to Blicker to avoid the worst shallow spots. Blicker kept looking back at the stern every time it sounded like the prop hit sand. Somehow, we got across the bay without running aground.

Another cut mysteriously appeared in the wall of mangrove trees. The hole was just big enough for the boat to pass; then it sealed over like it was never there. I looked back and searched the tangled mangrove limbs, but the opening had vanished.

Georgene and I ducked branches as the boat bored deeper and deeper into the little channels and creeks of the Sugarloaf backwaters. The sun barely pierced the covering trees. The water lay flat and oily, nearly lifeless, except for clumps of floating bugs. We wound a snarled path through the twisting jungle maze. For the first twenty minutes or so, I tried to track our course; but after a while I gave up, resigned to the fact that there was no possible way I'd be able to remember all the turns we'd made.

With only the rumbling engine and the occasional crying bird to break the silence, I peeked over the side and told myself the scary truth: There was nobody here.

I searched Georgene's face. She looked back at me, clearly terrified.

My chest suddenly tightened at the sight of another boat in the shadows ahead of us.

As we got closer, I stared past the snarled branches at the boxy boat floating low in the water. A houseboat.

Our old fishing boat crept down the final stretch of the clogged waterway. We pulled in close, and Blicker lashed up to a rusted cleat. Vic bounded onto the low deck with a flat metallic thud, and the pontoon boat jounced up and down on the line.

Georgene squeezed the fingers on my right hand. I could feel the pain, but I didn't react. I was too busy looking at the men and the shadowy jungle.

14

WITH OUR HANDS STILL tied behind our backs, we were herded across the deck of the rusted-out houseboat. We stumbled over battered crates and hoses and scattered engine parts to get to the door. Horrible thoughts jockeyed around my mind as I wondered what was coming next.

"Move it, kid!" Blicker ordered. Georgene nudged me toward the ragged screen door. I inched forward until Vic suddenly pushed past me and yanked the door open. Then he shoved me inside.

The small, dark space was cluttered with crates and equipment. Even in the gloom, I could see the grime on the cook top in the cramped galley along the back wall. My nose wrinkled at the stale stench of bacon fat.

Vic hauled us across the tiny room, clunking Georgene's head against the metal rim on the old formica table as he shoved her down.

"Ow! You don't have to push, I'm going!" she said.

He motioned for her to get under the table.

Seconds later, I hunched beside her.

Georgene poked her head out. "My dad's looking for us. He's got the Marine Patrol and the Coast Guard out by now. This is *kidnapping!* You better let us out of here!"

"Shhh!" I pulled her back under the table. "They don't care, Georgene. Stay still."

"You two just keep it shut." Blicker aimed a thick finger at us.

We huddled together, and I forced the lump back down my throat.

Blicker's eyes cut over to Vic. "All right, Purcell's not here. I better head to the other site and tell him what's up."

"You're not about to talk to Purcell without me there—" challenged Vic.

"Suit yourself. We'll both go. But first we'll drop this haul in the box out there on the deck. No need for us runnin' round with all that metal."

Halfway out the door, Blicker turned back and barked out, "Vic—use those lines. Make sure those two are tied extra-tight so they stay put. Find something for gags, too. Don't want them yellin' their fool heads off, even if there's not a live body anywhere near this hole. Make it quick. Then get on out here'n help me move this stuff."

Crashing sounds outside made me assume Blicker was heaving blocks into the bin we'd passed. Georgene and I huddled under the table, flinching at each heavy crash. Vic never even glanced up as he tied us. Grunting, he forced us to sit back-to-back and then bound us to the table leg. He pulled the rope so tight it cut into my wrists. He jumped to his feet and something slipped out of his pocket. The blade sprang open when the long-handled knife hit the deck.

Vic scooped it up off the floor. My eyes tracked the flashing blade as he waved the knife in front of my face. I gasped, trying not to choke on my spit.

"Chad, are you okay?" Georgene asked.

"Quiet!"

Vic crouched down next to me and held a finger to his lips. "Keep it shut, or I'll fix it so you can't make any noise. If it was me callin' the shots, I'd get rid of the both of you right now. You get me?" He glanced at the door, snapped the blade shut, and tucked the knife back in his pocket.

A sneeze scratched up the back of my nose. "*Achoo!*" Droplets sprayed the side of Vic's face.

"Watch it!" he snapped. He pulled away and smeared the slime off his cheek.

"Achoo. *ACHOOO!*" I couldn't stop, but I aimed away from him this time.

Vic twisted rags into long strips. He gagged me first, and then Georgene, muttering as he worked. "This'll keep you two quiet till we get back." Then he lunged to his feet and headed outside.

Unable to move and barely able to breathe, I fought down panic. I felt Georgene's shoulders shaking; she was crying.

These men are going to do whatever it takes to keep their stolen treasure, I thought. Georgene and I were just in the way. Maybe this time I'd gotten us into something we weren't going to get out of.

Breathe, Chad, I told myself. *Even though there's a nasty rag jammed in your mouth. Just breathe through your nose—and don't choke. Stay calm.*

Think about something good.

Is Dad back from Key West? I wondered. *Does he even know we're missing?*

Outside, the rumbling voices suddenly got louder; then they quieted down, and I could only hear some of what they were saying.

"... Purcell ... rid of ... kids somehow."

"he'll ... with ... plan?"

"... boat lined up ... night ... new site ... loaded ... silver ... just see ... blast ... reef ... right there ... other charts."

I bumped Georgene's shoulder. She pushed back.

"Don't want ... nothing till ... talk to Purcell ... no way ... change ... know ... to them."

Slow breaths, Chad. Slow breaths, I chanted in my head.

Minutes later, I heard the heavy lid slam and then hollow footsteps clomp across the deck. Finally, the engine puttered quietly out the channel.

15

ONCE THE DEEP RUMBLE faded away, Georgene butted me again.

"Mmhh, mmhhh," she grunted through the thick rag.

Tied back-to-back, it wasn't easy to help each other. Georgene angled her head at me trying to tell me something. "Mmhh, mmh, nnll, ih, agh."

I arched my back, stretching my fingers to pull at the lumpy rope around her wrists. I worked at it a while until finally the knot opened just the slightest bit.

Okay.

Squeezing and pressing, I stuffed the frayed line back through the main knot. I wiggled the snarled nylon back and forth as I inched it open enough to slide it off Georgene's hands.

I felt her shoulders moving for what seemed like a very long time. I hoped she was getting the gag out of her mouth.

"You did it!" she finally cried out. "Ahhh. There's pins and needles all up my arms."

I shook my head and grunted.

Untie me now, I silently begged.

"Okay, okay. I'll get to you. I just need to get my legs untied."

Over my shoulder, I saw Georgene pull herself to her feet and hop over to the counter. Stopping in front of two small drawers, she yanked one open, and with a jangling crash, an army of rusted kitchen utensils scattered across the floor.

What are you doing? They could be back any minute, I screamed in my head. I'd been hearing imaginary engines the whole time.

The guts of a second drawer clattered over the counter. Georgene dug through the flatware, flinging useless spatulas and spoons left and right.

"Got it!" she cried, holding up a pointed screwdriver. She worked it into the knot tying her feet. One end came loose; she pushed it back through the opening enough to slide it off her feet. She rubbed her ankles and smiled at me.

All I could do was grunt and shake my head at her.

"Okay. Okay. I'll get you untied!"

Once she had the gag off my face, I could breathe normally, which made me feel a whole lot calmer.

"You okay?" Georgene asked, her voice shaking a little.

I nodded. She used the screwdriver to untie my hands and feet. I swiveled my sore wrists around and rubbed at the raw skin. We hadn't been tied very long, but I still needed to pump my arms and legs to get the blood flowing.

"Did you hear what they said?"

"Some of it. We gotta get out of here. That guy, Vic—the big smelly one with the knife—wants us gone."

"They both do."

"We're in the middle of some kind of, I don't know, treasure looting operation. I thought I heard them saying something about blasting. Something about the reef . . . so they can find more treasure. We're in the way."

Georgene was halfway to the door. "Come on. They'll be back. We gotta get out of here, now!"

Blinking and squinting in the bright light, Georgene scurried for the ladder. I caught her elbow and squeezed. "Wait. We need a sample of the stuff they took. The rocks and coins, I mean. We need proof for the police."

Georgene yanked her arm free. "I don't *care* what they stole. I just want to get out of here!" She stepped down onto the rickety boarding ladder.

"But *wait*. We have to do something, now. It's still pretty early. You heard them talking about blowing something up. How can we not turn them in?" I slammed the lid of the wooden bin open and started digging around in the blocks of coins.

"*No!* Nobody will have a chance to care why we went back if we don't get away first. Somebody else can catch those guys later."

Suddenly remembering they'd towed our boat here, I looked around. "Where's the skiff?"

"I don't know. They must have towed it off again. Let's just *go*—" Before I could answer, Georgene had scrambled over the pontoon and down the rickety ladder. "Hurry," she urged.

I bent over the bin and pushed aside some of the larger blocks until I found some smaller chunks of rock that I figured I could carry. I pulled a crumpled cloth bag out from under a beach chair and dumped the crusted coins in the bag.

Georgene struggled to keep her footing in the knee-deep water as she headed out of the shallow creek. I slung the blocky sack over my shoulder and slid down the ladder, plunging into soft muck. My feet churned up little clouds of mud from the squishy bottom. Clumps of spongy grasses clung to my ankles and calves with each step.

We were far back in the jungle in a maze of shadowy creeks. I peered ahead, but with the thick screen of mangroves, it was hard to tell which way to go. Feeling eyes watching me from the shadows, I kept moving.

16

I LET OUT A SHAKY breath as we waded into a clearing. Completely disoriented about what direction we had gone, I studied the afternoon sun.

"Which way do you think they went?" Georgene said quietly.

"I don't know. They were going to find that other guy, Purcell, wherever he was," I shrugged.

We made our way through the thick brush, away from the houseboat. At the end of that stream we turned down another slightly wider canal.

"This isn't the way they brought us here, is it?" I said.

"I don't think so. The sun's over there now, so we should be moving away from the lagoon we crossed to get to the house boat."

We kept moving, but it was slow going with the thick underbrush. After another ten minutes, I saw an opening in the mangroves up ahead of us.

"Gene, look!" With my hand shading my eyes, I thought I saw a stream of water in the opening.

As we got closer, I realized it was a channel unlike the canals behind our house. This was more like a little river flowing through the jungle. I hoped maybe it would cut across the island and lead us away from where the men had brought us.

I shoved aside the wall of brush and started bushwhacking through the wiry branches. It took both of us to move some of the thickest limbs as we half-walked, half-crawled toward the water. We battled the tangled branches for another forty yards and ended up in a small clearing that I was sure we hadn't been in before. The sun beat down on us as we stood at the edge of a ledge about eight feet above the water. Mangroves roots grew out of the mud banks below us.

Before I knew what was happening, Georgene was falling—or maybe she had leaped—off the steep bank.

"Gene!" I grabbed for her, but she plunged into the flowing water and disappeared.

Jump in, the voice in my head said.

But I just stood there looking at the spot where she'd gone under.

Just then, a matted clump of dirty-blonde curls corked up a few yards down the little river.

"Jump in, Chad!"

"Maybe we should hike along the edge of the canal," I said, but then I saw the thick tangle of mangroves clogging the banks. But how would I be able to swim with the heavy bag of rocks? I hesitated, watching my sister drift slowly toward a tight bend to the left, when another fear suddenly shot to the top of the thoughts churning in my mind: *Where are Blicker and Vic?*

I dumped half of the rocks out of the bag. Then I held it tight to my chest and jumped down into the water. I kicked back to the surface. Paddling with one hand so I could hold the bag in the other, I swam over to Georgene and eventually paddled past her.

I could only imagine what might be down below me in the dark water.

"Can you help with this bag, Georgene? I took some of the rocks out, but it's still heavy," I said.

"Forget the bag," she said. "We've got to get out of here as fast as we can."

"I'm not leaving it."

Georgene swam faster and caught up with me. "Okay, fine," she said, and grabbed the other strap on the bag.

We struggled along, side by side, each stroking with a free hand.

"I can't see more than five inches down," she said a few minutes later.

"I know."

"Chad, do you think alligators come back in here?"

"Stop, Gene. Please—just swim, okay?"

I couldn't stop the thought that had flashed in my mind since we left the houseboat: *We are swimming through some middle-of-nowhere canal trying to get away from treasure thieves who want to get rid of us.*

Georgene and I drifted quietly for ten more minutes. Then we slid around another narrow bend where the banks sloped sharply upward.

The light brightened.

17

I SQUINTED UP AT PATCHES of brightness. We drifted in sunlight for a few minutes and then slid back into the shadows under a thick canopy of trees.

My eyes adjusted to the dim light, and I inhaled sharply.

Snake.

Just ahead of us, coiled on a branch eight or nine feet above our heads, a snake slept in a patch of sunlight. Mottled brown, with no distinguishing markings that I could see, it looked to be about four feet long, but it was hard to tell for sure the way it was curled up like that.

I held my breath and didn't take my eyes off of it. *Please be a harmless water snake.* I glanced at Georgene, who was focused on the water ahead of us. I was sure she hadn't seen it.

Don't look up, don't look up. I kicked hard to steer Georgene off to the left. I figured we could just slip past it if we stayed quiet and moved quickly, so I paddled harder, trying not to make any noise.

But then, Georgene spat out a big spurt of water. She whacked the water with noisy slaps as she struggled to paddle with the heavy bag.

"Shhhh," I hissed and grabbed the bag from her.

As we slid below the snake, a heron exploded out of the bushes, enormous wings flapping for the sky. I looked up just in time to see the startled snake uncoil smoothly and slip off the branch, smacking Georgene's shoulder blade as it hit the water with a splash.

"Eeeeeek!"

The snake circled her shoulders, and Georgene's arms spun wild as she heaved back, frantically trying to get away.

"Ahhhh! Chad! Get it off! Get it!"

She lurched away from me in panic; I went under for a moment as the bag dragged me down. I choked and coughed once I got my head out of the water.

Georgene flapped like a chicken, moving farther away from me as she jerked and clawed at the water.

"Hang on, Georgene!" I choked.

Two big scissor kicks got me closer, but then, with a couple feet still to go, I watched in horror as, with lightning-fast speed, the snake arched back and struck Georgene's arm. Then it slipped into the water and was gone.

Ahh-eeee!

Georgene heaved back, clutching her arm. She dropped below the surface of the murky water for a moment. Then she popped back up. Fighting to stick her nose in the air, she took a huge swallow of water instead.

"Georgene!" I lunged for her hair—just as the bag slipped off my shoulder.

"Cha-a-a-d!" Georgene screeched, and sank below the surface.

I reached for her, but I couldn't see a thing. I kicked down, blowing bubbles as I dove, and frantically swept my arms back and forth. Nothing.

Where is she?

I fought back up, choked in another gulp of air, and dove down again. This time, I snagged a clump of hair with my fingers. I kicked down a couple more feet, grabbed Georgene's arm, and pulled. Wild now, she thrashed and kicked as I pushed off the bottom and tried to swim up with her. Suddenly, she lunged up and clamped her arms around my neck. Tearing at my face and shoulders, she climbed me like a tree, dragging us both back down.

I heaved back and pushed her away with my foot. I needed air! I grabbed her arm and fought for the surface.

I popped up, choking and spitting. Kicking hard to stay up, I finally hauled my sister up too, but she wasn't moving. When I yanked her head up, it flopped back down. I smacked her cheek with the back of my hand.

"Georgene, breathe!" I yelled, slapping her again and kicking as hard as I could to keep the two of us above water. Her head suddenly heaved back, and she puked up a big gush of water. She coughed and hacked and gulped in air all at the same time.

"Easy, take it easy. Just breathe! It's gone. Relax so I can get us over to the side!" I ordered. Georgene kept choking and sputtering, but she relaxed enough so I could drag us both over to the side. I grabbed a mangrove root sticking out of the steep bank and hung on, still trying to catch my breath.

Georgene spat out more water. Finally, she dragged in a couple of shaky breaths. I shifted my grip and pulled her out of the water as much as I could. Tears streamed down her pasty face, and her bloodshot eyes searched mine as she sucked in more air. She finally stuttered, "I c-c-c-ouldn't g-g-get *air!*"

"Breathe, Genie. You're okay. Just breathe."

"It ... bit ... me."

"I know. Take it easy. Just a water snake, not poisonous. Guess we shook it up."

"Shook *it* up? Wh-what about me?"

I stared into Georgene's eyes, not really sure what I was looking for. Her pupils seemed okay. Both eyes were red but pretty focused. "You okay, now?"

She seemed to be getting air a little more easily. I grabbed her arm to check on the snakebite.

"Ouch. Take it easy."

"Sorry."

There were rows of red marks and a little blood, but no real bite that I could see—and no real swelling. Nothing like that.

"I think it'll be okay, Gene," I reassured her, trying to remember what I'd learned about snakebites at sea camp and hoping I was right.

"But it kills," she whimpered.

"Yeah, but I don't think there's any poison. We gotta keep moving. Think you can swim now?"

Georgene shuddered. "Don't know. Need to rest."

We didn't really have time to rest, but I knew Georgene was too weak to go on just then. "Okay, we'll wait a few minutes."

I clung to the mangrove root and tugged Georgene's head and shoulders a little higher. Breathing heavily, I scanned the water behind us. The ripples we'd churned up were dying out. The water lay flat and dark once again. An eerie silence hung in the air.

18

WHEN WE WERE BOTH calmer and breathing easier, I grabbed Georgene's good arm and started towing her back out to the middle of the canal. "Come on, Gene. We need to get out of here. I can pull you for a while. Just float. I'll tow you." With Georgene sprawled across my hip, I side-stroked awkwardly.

A small voice asked, "Think I'll be all right?"

"Yeah," I huffed, wondering what kind of snake it was. I really had thought it would just swim away. It happened so fast. I spat salt water, imagining what lay ahead of us as I swam with the tide.

Georgene craned her neck to look at me. "Where's the bag? Where're the coins?"

"I dropped it when I went after you. It's on the bottom."

"But won't we need it? For proof?"

"Can't help it. Too heavy to tow. It's on the bottom. Back there," I said, breathing heavily. "Somebody'll have to get it later . . . if we ever get out of here."

"You think those guys are around here somewhere?"

"Forget them," I said, trying to sound confident even though I was worried about the exact same thing. "We'll get out of this hole." The muscles in my legs burned. Working hard, I struggled along with Georgene.

We moved along pretty quickly for a while, but we slowed way down when the current died out. My left leg suddenly came up to my chest as a sharp spasm shot through my instep. Bent in two with the pain, I stopped swimming and tried to knead the arch of my foot while I hung onto Georgene.

"What's the matter, Chad?" Georgene said, her voice still hoarse and shaky.

"Nothing. Foot's just tired," I lied, wiggling my foot to try to ease the cramped muscles as we drifted farther down the canal.

"I'll swim," Georgene offered.

I knew she couldn't keep herself moving yet, and no way was I going under for her again, so I said, "No, Gene. It's okay. You just stay still. I've got you."

I hauled her on my other hip, and the pain in my foot gradually eased up. I paddled steadily, using the current as much as I could. "Hang on, Gene. We're okay," I coached, reassuring myself as much as her.

She managed a little smile, but she still looked pretty bad. "Thanks, Chad. Thanks for saving me."

"Oh, man. Look . . . I'm sorry, Genie. I'm sorry I got you—us—into this mess to begin with. I just . . . I had no idea."

"I know, Chad," she said, quietly. "Forget it. We're gonna get out of here."

It was the first time I'd admitted that I was responsible for this. I'd been trying to push it out of my mind the whole time we'd been swimming, but it kept churning in my head and gut. It surprised me how much better I felt once I'd admitted it out loud.

Paddling wearily, I admitted to myself that we needed help. I was so tired; it was hard to keep Georgene's face out of the water. I pulled her around another wide bend. In the spooky quiet, insects buzzed—the only sound.

Eventually, we coasted out to the edge of a small sunny bay. A faded wooden boat floated in the still green water. Straw hats shaded the faces of several men pulling in the small boats that were tied at the stern.

"No. Oh, no." Georgene's head was up. She eyed the men anxiously and tried to pull me back, but she had no strength. "What if they're the guys Blicker and Vic went to find? Don't let them see you."

I glanced at her before I turned back toward the boat. "Gene, they're sponge fishermen. We've seen them poling around, spearing sponges in our bay."

"But we don't know who's on that boat."

I told her that I'd seen them that morning in our bay on Cudjoe, and that I'd had the exact same thought she'd just had. We watched a little longer. "I think it'll be okay. I don't see those guys."

"Can you really tell?" Georgene hung draped over my shoulder. "I can't see who they are. . . ."

"Come on, Genie. We need help," I coaxed, gently pulling her along. "These guys are probably just sponge fishing." I looked back at the men, hoping I was right.

19

DRAGGED BY THE CURRENT, we slid across the open water and finally slowed to a stop not far from the sponge boats.

Perfect. No place to hide.

Two fishermen stood at the bow, long poles stabbing the clear water. Crouched in the cockpit, a third man tossed sponges into the closest dinghy. Behind the lead boat, three more small boats tugged at their lines. They looked just like the boats I'd seen back in our bay. But now, each skiff rode low in the water loaded down by mounds of waterlogged sponges.

"Should we go closer?" Georgene said.

"Maybe they can help us, Gene," I said, still trying to reassure her, as I looked around hoping to spot another boat—any other boat.

"Where are we? I don't recognize any of this."

From the lead boat's stern, one of the men spotted us. "*Miralos,*" he called to the other fishermen. One by one, the men turned and stared at Georgene and me.

"*¿Necesitan ayuda?*" asked the nearest man, poling his sponge-loaded skiff over to where we bobbed in the water.

We definitely needed help. I nodded my head.

"Come on, Gene." I tugged at Georgene's arm, dragging her along as I paddled closer. "We don't have any choice. There's nobody else here, and we need help."

The fisherman reached down and helped me climb into the little boat. Georgene held back for a moment; then she reached up with her good arm, and the man lifted her in. She flopped on top of the sponges and huddled next to me.

Once the fisherman had poled back to the main boat, a squat scowling man met us at the rail. His dark eyes observed us from under thick eyebrows.

"You are hurt? Climb in." He pronounced each word carefully, with a heavy accent. The muscles along his jaw clenched and unclenched as he glanced back at the other men. Then he reached over the side, and with a small grunt of effort, swung first me, then Georgene, up into the sponge boat.

Georgene's eyes moved from one man to the next. Looking for Blicker and Vic—just like I was. From the shade of their straw hats, the men silently stared, and I wished we were some place else.

The thought played over and over in my head like a stuck disc as I made a promise to myself: If, by some miracle, we manage to get out of this mess, I won't ever get obsessed with treasure or any other kind of adventure again.

Ever.

Georgene scooted closer to me. Suddenly fascinated by her feet, she studied the puddles at her toes.

I took the wet bottle from the Captain's outstretched hand and slung it up quickly downing three huge gulps of cool water. "Thanks," I grunted, and passed the bottle to Georgene.

The Captain searched my face and then Georgene's. "The radio, it says Marine Patrol, they are looking for two lost kids. South side of Sugarloaf Key—*esta mediodia.* You are these missing *niños*, no?"

I nodded, croaking out the words, "Yeah, that's us. They kidnapped us."

He pointed to the red marks on Georgene's upper arm. "What happened?"

Georgene wrapped her fingers over the horseshoe-shaped marks, but kept her mouth shut.

"Snake bit her. We scared it," I said.

The captain bent closer; Georgene pulled back, but then she moved her hand and let him study the marks. "I see no . . . ah, what you say, poison. No marks of the fangs. No, no poison," he mused. He signaled to one of the crewmen, who ducked inside the pilothouse and returned with a small plastic box that he set down next to Georgene. The captain opened the lid, revealing common first aid supplies just like at home. He opened a package of disinfectant wipes and used one to clean his hands; then he took a fresh one and cleaned the bite marks on her arm. He pressed lightly, but Georgene still winced each time he touched her arm. Working quickly, he swabbed on some antibiotic ointment and covered the bites with a gauze pad and a length of gauze. When he had finished wrapping the gauze around her arm and securing it tidily, Georgene thanked him with a brief smile. Then she leaned back against the gunwale and closed her eyes.

"She's pretty weak," I told the captain. "I don't know if it's the snakebite or because she almost drowned back there in the canal." My voice still sounded shaky to me.

"I'll be okay, Chad. Just wanna get home," Georgene murmured weakly, without opening her eyes.

I knew she was trying to encourage me, so I blocked out the guilt that had suddenly come flooding back. I asked, "Can you take us back to Cudjoe Bay? We have to get help and we need to let our dad know we're okay."

The captain ducked his head with a slow, thoughtful nod. "Yes. We will take you to Cudjoe. We will be taking you to your father. My name is Ramirez, Diego Ramirez. And your names?"

"Chad. This is my sister, Gene . . . uh, Georgene."

The bright sun baked my clammy skin as I told the story. "Two men kidnapped us. They stole silver—silver treasure—from a dive site off Sugarloaf. We got too close. So they picked us up." I darted a look at Georgene before I went on. "They took us to a houseboat and tied us up. They were going to get rid of us—but we got away and the current in that canal carried us all the way across the island. I think Gene must've swallowed a gallon of salt water when that snake dropped on her. She's been really weak ever since."

I was relieved to see Georgene sitting up now, listening quietly as I told the rest of the story. "We had coins, in a bag, that those men stole—but we dropped the bag back in the canal."

Frowning, shaking his head, Captain Ramirez raised both hands, palms forward. "*Basta, silencio.* We must leave this place now. Rest."

"They're going back out there. Those men—they're stealing treasure," I rushed to explain. "They're going to move to another dive site. We have to get somebody to catch them."

He looked from me to Georgene. "We will take you to your father—he will decide what to do."

Captain Ramirez barked rapid commands in Spanish, and the fishermen scattered across the deck. One man hauled up the anchor while another tied off the skiffs with quick figure eights on the pitted chrome cleat. Towing the sponge loaded skiffs we slowly motored out of the little bay.

I slid down next to Georgene and nudged her good arm. "We're going home, Gene."

She managed a thin smile, but her eyes showed how exhausted she was.

The powerful old Mercury engine huffed and chugged a while and finally shuddered up to full speed. Ten minutes later, we swung around a point of land and rumbled on toward a marked channel I'd never seen before. I stood at the rail and stared at two medium-sized fishing boats cruising around another bend in the distance up ahead of us. I rubbed my twitching eyebrow and watched the boats speed toward us.

"Gene, what if those men show up again?"

Georgene's chin jerked up off her chest. "What?"

The captain glanced at Georgene and turned to look at the approaching boats far down the channel.

As I watched the lead boat, not ready to trust my own eyes, I turned to Georgene. "Tell me that's not Blicker and Vic's boat—"

"What is it you see?" asked Captain Ramirez.

"I think that first boat might be the men who took us before."

Georgene got to her feet. Leaning against the gunwale she watched the boats in the distance. "I can't tell, Chad."

As the boats moved around another bend in the channel, we got a pretty clear view. The second boat hung back just far enough to plow the smooth water at the center of the lead boat's wake. The first boat looked a lot like the old fishing boat that had taken us to the houseboat, but I'd never seen the second boat before.

"Stay low, Gene," I said, looking for a place to hide. I moved back behind the pilothouse and watched the small boats bobbing along behind us. They were packed with sponges and not big at all.

Captain Ramirez announced, "You will hide yourselves. If someone on that boat looks for you—we will stop them."

"I don't think ..." Georgene trailed off.

I looked back around the corner of the pilothouse. The boats were speeding closer by the minute. As I stood there debating what to do, I tried to ignore the question gnawing at me.

What if they stop this boat?

20

"**O**OOF!" The captain darted across the deck and hauled me back behind the wooden pilothouse. Then he looked back around the corner and stared down the channel. "You must stay in hiding for now."

I poked my head out. "Let me see."

"Get back!" he barked, pushing me out of sight.

He signaled to the stocky man at the wheel to slow the boat to a crawl. Next, he grabbed Georgene's hand and pulled her to her feet, guiding her toward the stern. Crouching down as best I could, I followed close behind.

"Get in." The captain nodded toward the sponge-loaded skiffs bucking over the wide wake.

"In the dinghy?" Not believing he really wanted us to climb down into the little boat, I shivered, my bony knees drilling the transom's weathered teak.

Georgene wasn't budging.

"If there is trouble, you must not be found," he insisted.

"Trouble?" Georgene whispered. She still didn't move.

The roar of the distant engines convinced me. "We should hide, Gene. There's no other place. Go, just in case." I tried to push her forward, but Georgene was stalled in first gear, like I was asking her to walk a gangplank into schooling sharks.

"Move," I hissed into her ear.

Georgene gripped the rail with both hands. She was swaying so much, I thought she would fall over. She shook her head, blinking rapidly, even as she hiked one knee up to the rail and whispered, "How are we going to fit in that puny dinghy with all those sponges?"

"They're coming, Gene!" I pushed her aside. "Snap out of it, would you? Grab the rope, *hurry*—" I yanked the towline and thrust it into her shaking hands and together we tugged at the line.

The chain of boats had barely moved five feet when the captain wedged between us. He grabbed the line with thick calloused hands and pulled, and the packed dinghies scooted in behind the lead boat. "Go! Get under!" he urged.

I sneaked another look at the boats, moving fast, but still far down the channel, as Georgene climbed over the rail. "Go, Gene," I coaxed.

She jumped down and landed awkwardly, and the little boat shot off over the rushing water. "Ow!" she cried as she hit the pile of sponges. "These things *kill*." Teetering on the lumpy sponges, she struggled for balance. I jumped down after her and grabbed her wrist.

Crab-like, we burrowed under the rough, smelly sea sponges.

"Ew!"

"Hurry! Get under."

We tunneled into the heavy, wet mound. "These things *stink*—and they're scratchy!" Once Georgene was totally buried under the wiry sponges, I dug past her thrashing feet.

"Quit kicking me! Hold still."

Riding dangerously low in the water, the small boat seesawed in the choppy wake. I settled into the sponges and listened as the approaching engines got louder. I couldn't hear anything from the crew, but I could feel the sponge boat was starting to pick up speed.

"Think they'll search us, Chad?"

"Why would they?" I said, fighting off the urge to cough. My head thumped dully as I strained to hear the approaching boats.

I heard one of the motors throttle back. The engine changed sound and I heard it getting closer. But then, a second boat suddenly roared past us.

No . . . oh, no.

"This tub's gonna take that wake hard," I warned. I groped around under the scratchy sponges and held on tight to the wood trim, as up and over, up and over, we sloshed across the wake.

Gradually, the wailing engine faded off. But another engine puttered steadily closer.

21

THE NEW ARRIVAL RUMBLED closer; I heard the sponge boat's engine throttle down. We weren't moving any more.

The little skiff bobbed in the water as we waited.

Suddenly, voices began shouting. I struggled to unscramble the angry words. I couldn't understand any of it.

Then, I heard a shot.

It was unmistakable—a single, very clear, gunshot; and the snarled voices suddenly stopped.

I could hear one of the voices clearly now.

"I think it's Blicker," I whispered.

I could hear him barking commands at the fishermen. Noisy threats, Spanish mixed with English, came back even louder. Again, there were too many voices. Too much yelling.

"What are they saying?"

"The spongers are trying to stop the other guys from boarding their boat," Georgene whispered.

The voices stopped. I heard locker doors screech on rusted metal tracks. Hatch covers cracked against the deck.

"They're searching the sponge boat," I whispered.

My nose itched and burned from the musty sponges. I needed air.

A voice yelled out, "Look back by the engines! Those kids could fit just about anywhere."

Georgene jammed her heel into my ankle. Sweat slid into my burning eyes.

Loud footfalls pounded again.

The dinghy suddenly jerked forward. Roughly tugged, we lurched against the sponge boat's stern with a heavy thud.

I held my breath.

"There's nothing but sponges in there." The words filtered down through the sponges.

I heard Blicker's muffled roar. "Check anyway!"

I just had to breathe. I felt a scratchy tingle start up my throat. I choked down a cough.

Thunk.

I forgot my throat as inches to the left of my eyes, a slender, wooden pole slid down into the sponges and back out again. I was curled up as tight as I could make myself in the little boat. But I still felt like a whale in a fish tank.

Thunk. Thunk!

This time the pole hit the seat in the bow of the dinghy.

Captain Ramirez started yelling. I couldn't make out a word of it.

Vic yelled something. I heard the bamboo pole clattering over the sponge boat's deck. He must have thrown it down—at least, that's what I hoped.

"Forget this, Blicker!" Vic barked. "Nothin' but sponges."

There were loud footsteps.

Jammed against the side, my neck and shoulders throbbed. I realized then that Georgene wasn't moving—she hadn't moved since they tugged us up to the sponge boat.

Blicker's voice suddenly boomed, "Those kids are probably still wandering the alligator canals back on Sugarloaf. Let's go."

Minutes later, with a ragged stutter, an engine roared. It chugged back along the channel. The engine noise faded slowly and then hummed in the distance.

"They're gone."

Like a periscope, stiff hair caked with sand, my head poked above the sponges in time to see the old fishing boat far down the channel. "They're gone, Gene," I sighed, aching and miserable. I started gulping down fresh air. Finally free of the dank sponges, I coughed and sneezed again and again.

When I realized that Georgene was still buried under the sponges, I dug down and pulled. As soon as her face hit the air, her eyes flew open and she spat out a mouthful of sponge dust. She coughed and choked, just the way I had, until she got some clear breaths.

"You okay?" I asked.

"Better now," she finally wheezed. "I was sure they'd find us under there. I want to go home!"

"You are okay?" called the captain, towing us in. A crewman helped us climb back over to the sponge boat. Georgene was still coughing as she crumpled to the deck.

The captain shook his head. "Those men were going to take you."

Slumped against the gunwale, all I could do was nod.

22

"RELEASE THE SKIFFS." One of the men climbed down into the first little boat. Another crewman untied the line and threw it. The dinghies drifted over to the edge of the channel, and the man started poling the string of boats back along the shallows.

"We need to be less heavy," Captain Ramirez said quietly. He swung the old boat around and revved the engines. He pushed the throttle forward and we started along the channel.

Totally turned around, I raised myself up higher and looked up and down the channel. I was trying to figure out which way we were headed. It took me a couple seconds to realize we were following the red markers along the right side of the channel. I knew we were headed back in, away from where the fishing boat had just gone.

"Captain Ramirez, you're following the red channel markers."

"Yes. Red, right, return," he said, with a tense smile.

Red, right, returning," I echoed dully, repeating the boating rule I'd heard a million times before. "You follow red channel markers—on the right side of the channel—to *return* . . . return to land, isn't that right?"

The captain nodded.

"We're going back in? This takes us back to Cudjoe Key?"

"Yes. I will take you to your father. This channel will go to Cudjoe," he replied, carefully steering the heavy boat past another marker.

Georgene silently glanced at me as the captain continued.

"You see, in these waters, in the Florida Keys, if you are *outside* the channel, then the markers can mean something different. A captain must know the exact location—where he is, and where he is headed—to stay on course."

"*Right*, but . . ." While he'd been explaining the intricacies of Florida's boating rules, I'd been looking down the channel, trying to decide. I'd never wanted to go home more than I did just then, but . . . "But if we don't track those men right now, they'll get away. Even if we report them, no one will find them." I had my eyes locked on Georgene as I said it.

She shook her head furiously. *No.*

"But what about the treasure? And they're going to damage the reef! After everything we've been through, how can we let them get away now?"

Slumping a little, my sister stared down the channel in the direction of the long-gone boats. She stood there a few moments, taking slow, deep breaths. Then she turned back to me, and I wondered at the changed expression in her eyes. "You're right. There's no way they're going to get away with this. Not after what we've been through."

"You sure?"

"Call the Marine Patrol," she said, setting her jaw.

I smiled at her for a second before getting to my feet. I went over to the pilot station and tapped the Captain's arm. "Captain Ramirez, the men went that way." I pointed back in the direction they'd gone. "I know we asked to go to Cudjoe—but those men will get away. We have to follow them, *now*, or we'll lose them."

Captain Ramirez searched my face. "That is not for us to worry about right now. Sit down, drink the water. Ramon, check the girl's arm once more."

Ramon came over to inspect Georgene's arm as another man handed us paper cups of water and a bag of chips. I drank some water and tore open the chips, taking a few before I passed the bag to Georgene.

We were still moving down the channel toward Cudjoe. I volunteered, "I think I know where those men are headed."

The captain swiveled in his seat eyeing me for a moment before returning his gaze to the water ahead of us. He guided the boat around the last marker, slid the throttle back, and let the boat glide to a standstill at the entrance to the channel.

The gunmetal-gray patrol boat had the words *Florida Marine Patrol* lettered on its hull. The twin 225 Yamaha engines suddenly throttled back, and rumbled steadily as the powerful Mako cruiser settled in the water. With a smooth spin of the wheel, the driver slid the boat alongside us.

I stared as a tall, deeply tanned man in a charcoal-gray shirt and matching pants stepped to the rail. From the shadow of his black cap, his mirrored aviator glasses glinted at us. "Who is in charge of this boat?" he demanded. "Over here, now." Captain Ramirez came out of the open pilothouse.

The officer looked at me. "Is your name Hatcher? Chad Hatcher?" he asked, in a friendlier tone.

I nodded quickly.

"Are you hurt, son? Is this your sister?"

"Yes, but, officer—I mean, no, I'm not hurt," I said nervously. "I'm Chad . . . and that's my sister, Georgene."

Gene appeared at my side.

"All right, son, you and your sister are safe. That's our first priority. My name is Officer Dan Marley. We'll take these men in and get you back to your father. He's real worried about the two of you. Officer White, take care of those men," he ordered, pointing toward the crewmen.

A second officer, younger than the first, hopped over to the sponge boat and headed down the deck toward the sponge fisherman.

Captain Ramirez spoke quietly, "Officer, this boy and this girl were trying . . ."

Officer Marley reached out and clamped a hand on the captain's shoulder. "You just stay quiet. You men are in serious trouble here."

His eyes becoming shiny black pellets, Captain Ramirez stood tall, while the other sponge fisherman hung back, nervously staring into the water.

23

THEY HAD IT ALL wrong.

"No, Officer, *wait*," I grabbed his arm. "That's not what happened. The men who stole the treasure ... the ones who took my sister and me—"

"Treasure? What are you talking about, son?" asked Officer Marley.

An engine whined. We all turned to watch as another boat flew around the bend in the channel, heading right for us.

"Hey Mike! Officer White!" yelled Turner as he swung the sleek Pursuit C 230 up to the patrol boat.

I waved to him and my eyes swept over the impressive boat. This was nothing like the little flats boat Turner usually ran around in. This boat was *fast*. A center console cruiser, it had been rigged for fishing and diving, with plenty of custom rod holders and a row of air tanks strapped along the gunwales.

"Hey, Turner," Officer White and I called out, at the same time.

"Chad! You guys okay?" Turner slid his sunglasses up on his hat and grabbed the line the officer threw him.

"What brings you out here, Turner?" asked Officer White.

"Harry Parker, over at the marina. He was monitoring the radio and heard the call a while back from Chad and Georgene's dad. I just wanted to see if I could help track them down out here. Sure glad I ran into you guys," he replied, with a relieved smile.

I rushed over to the rail. "Turner, can you take us back to Cudjoe?"

"Hold on. Nobody's going anywhere." Officer Marley held his hands up. "Except back to headquarters so we can sort all this out," he added, looking from Turner to me. "Now, let me get this story straight. What's this treasure you're talking about?"

"The silver coins ... those men were stealing Spanish treasure—we think it's Spanish treasure—from an old dive site," I started to explain.

"So, these sponge fishermen were stealing silver coins?" Officer Marley frowned.

Georgene shook her head. "No, *no*. Not the sponge fishermen. They help—"

Officer Marley cut her off. "All right, now, you two. We'll see about all this back at headquarters." He motioned to the other officer and Officer White led the captain and the other sponge fishermen toward the pilothouse.

"You men, *inside*—sit yourselves down on that deck," ordered Office White.

I put my hand on Officer Marley's arm. "Please listen. These men helped us get away. They're not the ones you need to arrest!"

But he was already moving down the deck, talking over his shoulder as he went. "I need you to just sit tight there, son. I told you we'd get back to headquarters and get this sorted out. Gotta head there, right away," he said. He looked around for White, then realized the other man was busy with the men in the pilothouse.

Then he noticed Turner hanging onto the side rail there taking it all in.

"Turner, could you run Chad and his sister back to headquarters while we deal with these men? We'll be right behind you, just as soon as we get this sponge boat checked out."

Turner looked from Georgene to me and quickly nodded. "Sure. Come on Chad and Gene, I'll drop you off."

"*Wait!* Officer Marley," I said, following him down the deck again. "We need to go after those other men. They're going to wreck that reef!" I tried again, but, busy with the sponge fishermen and the boats, neither man was listening.

"Get going, son," ordered Officer Marley.

24

URNER JAMMED THE THROTTLE forward, and we sped up the coast toward Marine Patrol headquarters. Georgene and I shared the bench behind Turner as we flew along the smooth water.

"They wouldn't listen, Gene. I can't believe they thought Captain Ramirez had taken us."

"I know. I tried telling Officer Marley, too."

"How did everything get turned around so fast? What a mess. Those men, Blicker and Vic, will be gone for good by the time somebody tries to track them down."

Looking confused, Turner glanced back at us.

"We'll just have to tell the officers again. Make them listen to us," I said. "Soon as we get to Marine Patrol headquarters."

"They're bringing the Captain and his men in for questioning . . . that's not right!" said Georgene.

"We'll just have to fix it."

We rounded the point of land at the tip of the island and the radio suddenly squawked. Turner hit the volume, and a voice boomed out, "*Dive Deep, Dive Deep*, this is Skip; come back."

Turner tapped the throttle down and grabbed the receiver. "This is Turner on the *Deep Dive*. Hey, Uncle Skip, what's up? Over."

"Turner, I got a little emergency over here at Miller's Basin. I need you to high tail it on over here with those air tanks I just refilled. Over."

"Miller's Basin? Where we did those shallow dives last year? I remember it. Over," Turner replied.

"That's it. Over at the north end of the bay. How long before you can get here?"

Alarmed, Georgene's eyes darted to me and back to Turner.

"I just have to drop off Chad and Gene, and then I'll head out there."

"Drop off *who*?" barked the voice on the radio. "I'm not runnin' any taxi service. Get over here now and bring me those tanks! I got a dive party to outfit. Do you copy me? Over and out." The radio screeched again and went dead.

"Yeah, I copy," Turner muttered to himself as he jammed the receiver back in the cradle.

Georgene leaned over and grabbed Turner's arm. "Wait a sec, Turner—we have to get to the Marine Patrol station. Can't you just drop us off before you take the tanks to your uncle?"

"I would, Georgene, but you just don't disobey my uncle. When he gives an order, it gets done pronto—or else. You guys'll just have to ride with me for a few; then I'll get you over to the station right after," Turner said, pressing the throttle forward.

I thought Georgene's head would shake loose. She glared at me.

"Where's this basin, Turner?" I asked.

"Not far." He kept his eyes on the water ahead of us.

"There's no way we should be running around out here," Georgene said, quietly enough that only I could hear.

I looked back and forth between them. "Take it easy, Gene. Turner's going to take us back just as soon as we run the tanks to his uncle."

"What if those men are still around?"

I knew she was right.

"Hey, man," I said, yelling into Turner's ear over the engine noise. "Can't you just run us back in real quick?"

Turner stared straight ahead. "Sorry. Really. This won't take long." He bumped up the throttle, and the powerful, direct-injected engine catapulted the heavy boat up on plane. It was impossible to talk over the racket.

Georgene set her lips in a tight line and watched the approaching island.

"Turner, we have to go back now," I called to him. I swigged down the last of the water I'd been drinking and tossed the bottle in the trash bucket. "After you left us this morning, Gene and I stopped at Wreckers Reef over on the south side of Sugarloaf. We weren't there five minutes before those guys showed up—the ones I told you were stealing the treasure at that dive site we checked out this morning."

Shouting to be heard, I told him about our escape as the Yamaha 250 hummed at nearly full throttle and we screamed over the sandy flats.

25

FIFTEEN MINUTES LATER, WE idled up to a shadowy green cut. Turner steered the boat through the narrow canal and we came out into an open bay.

"There it is." He pointed to the power cruiser anchored at the far side.

We sped across the little bay, and then slowed until we coasted up to his uncle's dive boat.

"Skip?" he called. "Hey, Uncle Skip!"

No answer. No movement on the boat. The only sound was a couple of water birds crying over our heads.

"What gives?" muttered Turner.

I stepped up on the gunwale, but Turner grabbed my arm. "Wait, Chad. I'll go."

He leaped across to the dive boat and disappeared inside the cabin. Seconds dragged by before he came outside again and hopped back across. He hit the deck with a grunt. "Skip's not there," he reported.

Georgene stared at the box in his hands. "What's that?"

I tilted my head to read the writing on the side. *Explosives.*

I let out a low whistle.

"Blasting material," Turner answered.

Georgene gave a little scream.

Turner angled the box forward so she could see inside. "It's okay. It's empty, see?"

"What's your uncle doing with that stuff?"

"Not sure. Uncle Skip worked commercial salvage for years, I know. He knows all sorts of stuff about demolition and explosives. I've heard sometimes treasure salvors set explosives to speed up the search, so they can move the sand faster and uncover the treasure."

Georgene's eyes widened in fear. "What if those guys picked him up?"

"The guys who took us, you mean?" I asked.

"Yeah. Maybe they needed help—help setting the explosives."

I raked my fingers through my hair. "Earlier, at the houseboat, when Blicker and Vic were talking? You said you thought you heard them talking about blowing something up."

"Skip must have been with them when he radioed me," said Turner.

"I wonder if he knew what they were up to then—" I hadn't meant to say it out loud. Georgene's startled eyes jumped from me to Turner.

But he only said, "Let's get moving." He slid over to the controls and pushed the throttle forward. My eyes burned, and my head ached as we raced back the way we'd come.

26

MINUTES LATER, WE CRUISED up to Wreckers Reef. Sloshing waves partly covered the rocks.

"There!" I shouted. "Over there!" Nearly blinded by the low position of the sun in the sky, I squinted at the glare on the water as I tried to make out any movement on the deck of the old fishing boat. It was anchored in just about the same spot we'd seen it earlier in the day.

Turner grabbed his binoculars and held them to his eyes. "Nobody's on deck. It's called the *Sand Dollar*," he said, reading the name off the stern. "They might be diving."

"We didn't see any air tanks before," I said.

Tuner shook his head. "But they're not coming up."

Standing at the rail, Georgene shaded her eyes with her hand. "Look." She pointed a little farther down the coastline. "There's a skiff anchored down there."

Turner aimed the glasses at the smaller boat. "Looks like they've got an airlift rigged up on there," he said.

"Like a pump, you mean?" asked Georgene.

I could see the boat if I squinted my eyes just right. "Treasure salvors use them to find stuff on the bottom of the ocean. They rig a pump to a long pipe and the diver uses it on the bottom like a vacuum to suck up sand and stuff."

"Like the hole in the sand at the bottom near the reef over there? The one you said you saw earlier today?"

"That's standard equipment for treasure salvage," agreed Turner. "I used one with my uncle before. There's the filter—that basket on the side of the skiff. That's where they strain out all the stuff they pump up and catch anything valuable they want to keep."

"We need to get a closer look," said Turner.

"Let's not get too close," Georgene urged.

"I'll do the looking. You two stay out of sight until we know what's going on."

"Get the Marine Patrol on the radio. We need them."

"They didn't listen to us before," I said, even though I agreed with her.

Turner made the call. He didn't bother to ask headquarters to locate the officers who'd stopped us earlier; he just asked the dispatcher to send the nearest patrol.

The engine rumbled quietly as we proceeded across the water. Once we got close enough, Turner killed the engine; we coasted the last hundred yards up to the *Sand Dollar.* I stared at the cabin's dark windows. Then I scanned the shadowy water one more time, wondering what else besides the reef the dark shadows might be hiding.

There was no sign of the men, so Georgene grabbed a line and lashed the boats together. Climbing aboard the other boat, Turner quietly circled the deck, then ducked inside the low pilothouse. Seconds later, he was back outside, holding up a *Deep Dive* T-shirt, size XXL. "It's Skip's shirt," he said, quietly. He also had a box of the same type of blasting explosives we'd found at Miller's Basin. "There's all sorts of equipment in there."

"Same stuff we just found at Skip's dive boat. Do you ..." I paused for a second, thinking it over. "Think ... maybe your uncle is in with them?"

"No way," snapped Turner. "He knows about salvage and blasting, sure, but that was before he started his dive business."

"I thought you said he worked treasure salvage, too."

"He did, but that was for a big outfit down in Key West. They're totally legit, everything by the book, I'm sure," he replied, not sounding sure at all.

"Blasting on a reef is definitely not by the book," said Georgene. Her eyes skimmed the water again. "Where are those guys? Maybe we should get away from here, at least until the Marine Patrol shows up."

"Skip would never do anything to harm his precious reef. He fishes and dives—he's a nut about protecting the marine sanctuary—the reefs and all the live coral."

Turner kept his voice low, but the tension in it was unmistakable.

"So why's he helping these guys?" I was asking the obvious question we'd all been avoiding.

"I don't have a clue." Turner's eyes were suddenly filled with doubt.

"*Unless* ..." Georgene began.

"Unless they're forcing him?"

"Did they really figure no one would come after them?"

Turner pulled up the lid of the storage bin on the fishing boat.

"Anything in there?"

He sighed. "Nothing."

"So, the silver's still back at the houseboat?"

"Either that, or that guy, Purcell, picked it up," I reasoned.

"Hang on. I think I saw something," said Turner, before darting back into the pilothouse.

Georgene moved over to the console. "I'm radioing the Marine Patrol again. We need help now."

"We already radioed, Gene. I just know those men are diving now. We've got to stop them!"

"We have to find them first!" she said, and grabbed the receiver.

27

TURNED AND MOVED TO the rail. "Stay here," I threw over my shoulder.

Georgene dropped the receiver and rushed over to me. "What? What are you doing?"

"I just want to check something out. Keep your eyes on the water in case I need to signal you, okay? Tell Turner I'll be right back."

Before she could talk me out of it, I hopped over the transom and slipped into the water. I breast-stroked silently through the glassy water until I reached the far side of the skiff. I climbed into the little boat.

Staying low, I studied the equipment. Boxes of blasting materials were stacked on the deck. The motor for the airlift hummed steadily. The curved pipe emptied into a wide catch basket that was partly filled with coins, sand, and blackened debris.

I couldn't see much, but I knew the men were down there somewhere. I had no idea how much air they had, or how long they could stay under.

Get it done, Chad.

Before I could lose my nerve, I shifted carefully to the other side of the skiff and shut off the airlift pump. I grabbed the wooden paddle and slid down below the gunwale.

Everything grew silent, except for the water lapping against the side of the skiff.

I didn't have to wait long. At first, just a few small air bubbles drifted to the top. Seconds later, little clumps of bubbles followed, one after the other.

And then, just below a big pool of them, I saw the diver swimming up.

He broke the surface with a splash and paddled toward the skiff muttering as he swam. "That blasted motor . . ."

The voice didn't belong to Blicker or Vic.

The diver dropped his fins into the skiff and hauled himself up the little dive ladder. "What the—!" He suddenly spotted me crouched in the bottom of the boat.

"Skip?" I said, quietly. "You're Turner's uncle, right?" The man wasn't tall, but he sure was bulky. Hunched over me like a wrestler ready for the take down, I figured he must have powerful muscles under all his blubber.

"What the devil are you doing out here?" he challenged. "Where's Turner?"

"Over there," I blurted, anxiously. "On the fishing boat with my sister. We followed those men, the ones stealing ..."

His shoulders relaxed. "Those two grabbed me back at Miller's Basin. They dragged me out here, not more than an hour ago—right after I radioed Turner—to engineer a blast for their salvage site." I cocked my head to the side. "They're forcing me . . . said if I didn't work with them, they'd rig it so I didn't come up. I was just going along with them long enough to find where they planned to set the explo—"

As if on cue, more air bubbles drifted to the surface.

"Stay down," he warned, a finger at his lips.

The diver surfaced with a quiet splash, and I ducked below the gunwale. Skip leaned over the airlift and fiddled with the switch.

"Get that thing cranking," barked a voice that sounded an awful lot like Vic's. My hands shook as I silently slid the wooden paddle out from under a pile of rope.

Skip stuck his hand back, signaling me not to move, as he replied, "It's jammed. I'm workin' on it. Give me some time here."

"You got exactly three minutes," growled Vic. He grabbed onto the gunwale, rocking the little boat as he hung on. "We got to sift through the rest of that section before you set the blast down there. It's near dark! Get that pump going—*fast*."

I jumped up and swung as hard as I could.

With a dull thud, the paddle connected with the side of Vic's head. He sank beneath the surface for a second before he started thrashing. I swung again, only this time

I wasn't so lucky. He yanked the paddle away from me and I flipped into the water.

Skip jumped into the water between Vic and me. He grabbed Vic around the neck, unclipping the buckle to his air tank. He pulled the tank and flotation vest off the other man. Still wearing the heavy weight belt, Vic started sinking fast.

Skip took a couple slow breaths treading water a few seconds before he swam down and dragged Vic back up. He hauled him to the skiff and dumped him over the side. Sprawled on the deck, Vic's chest heaved up and down, but his eyes stayed closed. He wasn't moving.

I climbed into the skiff and Skip followed right behind me. "That other guy's still down there," he panted.

"Is his name Blicker?" I asked anxiously, trying to catch my breath.

"No idea, kid."

"They're the ones who kidnapped us earlier today, but we got away. We saw them stealing treasure and they wanted us out of the way."

"True. They mean business. From what I heard, they been plannin' this haul a long time. They aren't about to give up easy."

I pointed as more bubbles floated to the top.

Someone else was coming up.

28

I TURNED THE KEY AND hit the throttle. The engine whined.

"Hold up a sec, got to get the anchor," cried Skip. Stepping to the bow, he grabbed a fish knife and sliced through the anchor line.

I hit the throttle harder this time, but we moved slowly given all the weight.

Suddenly, something zinged past my left ear. It hit the bow with a *thwack*, and I stared at the slender metal arrow lodged in the wooden post at the front of the boat.

"Get down! He's got a spear gun," Skip growled. "Hit that throttle, would you, kid?"

"I've got it full out!" Looking back over the stern, I spotted a pair of fins just as they slipped beneath the ripples.

"Didn't want to scare you back there . . . that animal is not playing around. I really thought I could stop them from blasting if I didn't make my move until they showed me the spot."

"Did they blow up anything?"

"Not yet, but they were getting close." He pressed down on my shoulder.

Minutes later, we slid around to the far side of the sleek Pursuit 230. Turner and Georgene hung over the rail.

"Stay low," Skip told them. "That guy's been shooting a spear gun at us."

Georgene dropped down flat on the deck. She let out a little gasp when she realized Vic was passed out in the bottom of the skiff. "Chad, are you okay?"

I nodded, but kept my eyes on Vic.

Georgene eyed me anxiously. "You sure you're okay? I can't believe you took off like that . . ."

Electricity still pumping through my veins, I let out a sharp laugh. Skip and I clambered onto the Pursuit.

Just then, I heard a new sound. A droning engine.

I sobered up fast as I watched the Marine Patrol cruiser slam across the open water.

"There they are—*finally*," Georgene said, relieved. "I radioed them again when you took off. They're hunting for Blicker and Vic. Searching for Purcell, too."

"Blicker's still down there somewhere with that spear gun."

The patrol boat rocketed over the last hundred yards, slowed, and circled back across the glaring water. It was clearly searching the area, traversing a section and slowly angling back to cover a path a few yards further east. Soon it slowed and came to a standstill, back-lit by the blinding late afternoon sun.

Looking over the rail, I strained to make out the people on the other boat. Dark outlines crouched over the dive ladder as they hauled someone into the boat. Seconds later, the police cruiser motored toward us.

At the rail, Turner glanced over at me. "Looks like they got the other guy."

As the custom Mako 26 slid nearer, I gaped at the man in the stern.

"That's Blicker," Georgene said, softly.

His mask and tank were gone. He was propped against the side, his hands cuffed behind his back. A massive officer guarded him while a second officer, a small blonde woman, piloted the boat.

"This one of your treasure suspects, Turner?" called the male officer.

"Are those the missing kids?" asked the female officer, pointing to me and Georgene. "Chad and Georgene Hatcher? Are you all right? Your father has been searching for you. My name's Officer Madsen, and this is Officer Brockett."

I nodded nervously, keeping my eyes on Blicker. "Does Dad know we're okay?"

"I'll get him on the radio now."

I took a slow breath and turned back to Skip. "We found that man, and the other guy in the skiff back there—his partner—stealing blocks of coins right here, this morning. They took us to a houseboat back in the jungle. It was in the middle of nowhere—somewhere in the backwaters on Sugarloaf."

With a grunt, Blicker started to claw to his feet, but Officer Brockett slapped a massive arm across his chest and he crumpled back down. "Just sit tight there. Don't move!"

Georgene and I rode with Turner for the trip back to headquarters. The patrol officers took Blicker and Vic, while Skip piloted the old fishing boat and towed the skiff.

As we motored toward the channel, an earsplitting roar suddenly split the air. I clamped my hands over my ears and watched the helicopter bank sharply. It charged back the other way, flying careful grids back and forth over the heavy canopy of trees.

When the racket died down Turner got on the radio with Skip. After a short exchange, he told us, "The Marine Patrol told Skip there's a big search on for that other guy you two were telling me about. Purcell, was that his name? That's why the helicopter. Not much light left, though."

I nudged Georgene and put my mouth up to her ear to whisper, "So Purcell's still out there somewhere. Blicker and Vic did the hauling, but I bet anything that guy, Purcell, got the rest of the treasure."

29

I T WAS ALMOST PITCH black when we pulled up to Marine Patrol headquarters on Summerland Key. Dad jumped into the boat, grabbed Georgene and me, and hugged us close. "I have been out of my mind about you two," he cried.

He led us to a bench at the side of the dock, and we all sat down. His eyes brimmed with tears. "Are you okay?"

The tension that had kept me going all day suddenly drained away. I sagged against him and smiled. "We're okay, Dad."

Georgene clung to his neck. Tears ran down her cheeks while she told him what had happened. "We got away from those men. A snake bit me back in the canal—"

Dad's eyes got wide. He shook his head but didn't say a word.

"I almost drowned . . . but Chad saved me," she whispered. His arm tightened around me as he buried his face in Georgene's hair.

"If the sponge fishermen hadn't helped—" I said. A huge lump in my throat kept me from finishing.

He pulled us in closer, talking quietly. "I couldn't believe it when I got back to the house and you'd both just vanished. I didn't even know you were gone until late this afternoon. I was tied up all day in that meeting and somehow missed the message the Baxter's left on my cell phone when they tried to check in with me."

"I had to go back out there, Dad. I saw them ... those men were stealing treasure. Nobody would believe us. I had to get proof."

"*Chad*—" Dad started.

"I just wanted to take another look, but then it all went so wrong." I stopped talking as the full impact of everything we'd been through came crashing down on me.

I realized then that Dad had been staring at my shorts.

He reached out and tugged at the blue lanyard hanging out of the side pocket on my board shorts. The flap that held the pocket closed ripped open then with a tearing sound as the GPS popped out. His eyes got big. He watched it swinging from the lanyard for a few seconds.

We looked at each other without saying a word.

I let out a shuddering sigh and waited.

I knew the worst had passed when he started to shake his head at me. Then, fighting the little smile that had appeared in the corners of his mouth, he pulled me close.

Georgene leaned over and rolled her eyes at me. "Only you, little brother," she said, grinning from ear to ear.

We spent the next ten minutes telling him everything. This time we didn't leave a thing out. Not even about the spear gun, or hiding under the sponges.

Before long, Officer Marley took us inside to the small room that doubled as an infirmary. They'd brought in a local doctor who checked out Georgene's arm and confirmed that the bite was just a nasty flesh wound—not poisonous. She gave us aloe lotion for sunburn and told us to get a lot of rest and drink lots of water, but she said, overall, we were both in pretty good shape, considering.

After the check up, Georgene and I had some orange juice and crackers before Officer Marley led us to another room at the back of the station. Several officers sat around a big wooden table.

"This is Chad and Georgene Hatcher, the kids who discovered the men looting silver out on the south side of Sugarloaf today," he announced. We sat down.

"Officer Marley, did you find the other guy?" I asked, hoping to hear he'd been locked up, too.

"No, not yet, son. He's still out there . . . but he'll turn up soon enough," Marley replied.

Captain Ramirez came into the room just then. Georgene and I shook his hand and thanked him. We rushed to tell the officers everything the sponge fishermen had done to help us escape that day. "We wouldn't be here now if it weren't for Captain Ramirez and his men," I finished.

This time, Officer Marley listened to me. Captain Ramirez showed the officers his licenses and permits for the sponge fishing boats. He wanted them to know he had all the proper documentation—especially his citizenship papers, of which he was obviously very proud. When he had finished his story, Officers Marley and White apologized to them, and also to Georgene and me, for the way they'd handled things at first.

It was a huge relief to finally to set the story straight.

As we told the officers the rest of our story, they asked so many questions that my head hurt even worse than it had all day. The thing they kept coming back to, the thing they had the hardest time understanding, was why we had gone back out to the reef in the first place. I tried to explain. I tried to make them understand that I had to find out about the treasure.

I had been so sure I was doing the right thing, but after everything that had happened to us, the only thing I was sure of, was that I wasn't sure of anything anymore.

30

THE NEXT MORNING I woke up clearheaded and hungry, hungrier than I'd ever been in my life. Dad made us French toast with real maple syrup for breakfast.

Then Georgene and I spent the rest of the day hanging around the house just taking it easy. Real easy. We ate everything we could get our hands on. If we weren't stretched out on lounge chairs out on the screened porch, we were digging around in the refrigerator for leftovers. I even made my specialty, peanut butter with honey & banana on toast, for an afternoon snack.

We ate, but we didn't talk—at least, not about what happened on Sugarloaf Key. I think Gene and I had silently agreed to stay away from that subject for the time being. Dad didn't bring it up, either. He didn't have to. Even without talking about it, I was having trouble keeping my mind off the danger I'd dragged us into the day before.

Still, it was a very good day.

For dinner, Gene and I made grilled cheese sandwiches and Dad made fresh tomato soup that was just about the best thing I'd ever tasted. By the time I put my spoon down, though, I was exhausted. I couldn't keep my eyes open.

"Wake up, Chad-man," Dad laughed. "You still need to rinse off. You're a sweaty mess after tossing that lacrosse ball at the wall out there two million times today. Go shower off. Then get right to bed, okay?"

I heard what he said, but I didn't have the strength to lift my head off my arms where they rested on the kitchen table. I opened my eyes just enough to let in a wedge of light. "I want to wait for Mom," I mumbled.

"She'll be here in the morning, I told you that earlier, buddy. Did you forget already?"

I yawned. "Mmm. Okay, Dad . . . g'night."

I stumbled across the kitchen and into the back bathroom, where I spun the shower faucet to H. Propping my arms against the tiles under the showerhead, I let the hot water pummel the sore muscles in my back and shoulders for a few minutes. Still almost half-asleep I started to towel off.

Just then, I heard quiet tapping at the front door. I tiptoed over to the open bathroom window and peeked through the blinds at the small landing. Two men waited under the weak light from the bug-bulb over their heads.

The screen door squeaked. Dad said, "Evening, Officer Marley. Please come in."

I pulled on a pair of shorts and an old Turtle Kraals T-shirt on my way back out to the kitchen. Squinting in the bright light, I saw Georgene and Dad had sat down at the table with the two men.

Officer Marley had brought a stranger with him. The man's close-cropped, dark, wiry hair had patches of gray at the sides. Owlish white circles around his eyes stood out in a sun-baked face. Black-bristled, his mustache fanned out above a friendly smile as I came closer.

"How are you feeling today, Georgene? Chad?" Officer Marley asked, giving each of us a little nod. "I hope you both got a good rest after your ordeal yesterday. You sure needed it."

"We're pretty good, thanks," Georgene replied.

I pulled out a chair and sat down next to Officer Marley. "We're doing better. Lot's better. Still tired, but it's great to be home." I covered my mouth as my smile stretched into a big yawn.

"That's good to hear. I hope you think twice before heading outside the channel on any more adventures." Marley smiled, but his tone was serious.

"I want to thank you again for bringing Georgene and Chad back safely, Officer," Dad said. "I still can't believe the trouble these two got themselves into."

"We were just glad it all turned out like it did." Officer Marley turned to me and Gene. "Well, guys, I have someone here who's anxious to meet you two." He gestured to the man sitting next to him. "This is Mr. Claude Panchet. He owns Deep Salvage, the company that held the old dive rights to the site where the treasure was stolen."

I looked over at Mr. Panchet expectantly. His dark eyes locked with Georgene's before swinging back to me.

"I heard all about what happened to you and your sister yesterday."

I nodded with a tight smile.

"First of all, I want to thank you both for your courage and quick action out there. You discovered the men looting at our old dive site, and with any luck, we'll be able to find the rest of the stolen coins. In the end, the lawyers will decide who claims the treasure, but you've alerted us to the looting, and I thank you for that."

I nodded again, relieved he had something good to say about what we'd done the day before. Georgene smiled.

"A trunk of old company charts was stolen a few years ago. We never found out who took them, but just yesterday, they found a couple of the charts on that old fishing boat the men were using."

"Apparently, Larry Blicker got wind of the stolen charts a while back," Officer Marley added. "We don't yet know how many people are working this looting scheme. But according to what we got out of that Blicker character so far, he's been involved with a looting operation up here around Sugarloaf for some time now. That houseboat where they took you two ... we believe it's just one of the hideouts they use to stash the stolen goods." He paused. "The story gets even more interesting, though. Skip Walker and his nephew brought in some of the same charts to show us. Turns out, Skip had them from years back. He was part of the dive team working legal claims owned by Deep Salvage back then."

"I saw those charts," I said. "Turner and I found them yesterday morning. That's why we went back out there."

"Turner told me, Chad. His uncle was not happy about that. You know you could have come to us right then? You didn't have to take off on your own out there."

"I just wanted proof. We weren't planning on going anywhere near those men but then the engine conked out on us—"

Mr. Panchet jumped in. "There have been looting incidents down off Key West. These same men you're holding up here may also be involved in what's happened down there."

"Your actions brought in two of the group," said Officer Marley. "Hopefully, we'll be able to identify the other looters and apprehend them as soon as possible."

"Are those sites in Key West inside the marine sanctuary too?" Georgene asked.

"Yes, Georgene," said Mr. Panchet. "In fact, some of them were old company sites of ours, and some from other treasure salvage operations. The sites close in to the reef are off limits now. We only dive legitimate sites with the proper permits."

"Do you still find treasure?" I spoke up.

"We certainly do. Things have changed quite a bit over the years, Chad, but the equipment and salvage techniques have only gotten better. You know, it's very expensive—and very slow going—to properly salvage treasure buried under the ocean floor. It can take many days and months, often years, of hard work. It's not just silver and gold and jewels, you know. There is much history to be learned from a shipwreck. We have marine archaeologists, experts in the science of marine exploration, to prepare the salvage site and properly identify everything we recover."

Officer Marley said, "That's one of the reasons we're so focused on the men you discovered. If they're part of the team that's hit the sites off Key West, we want them stopped. They do more damage than any storm we've seen. At one of the sites off Key West, the Marine Patrol found a thirty-foot crater on the ocean floor. Speculation is that explosives caused the massive holes, but we don't really know at this point."

"Did they find treasure down there too?" I asked.

"We're checking into it," said Officer Marley. "We don't know yet what they turned up down there."

My mind raced with questions. "If there never were any Spanish ship wrecks up this way, then how did all that treasure get up here? And what about the explosives? Did those men ever blast anything up here?"

Officer Marley shook his head. "No explosions that we know of. You stopped them, just in time, apparently. You caught up with Skip before they could set off the explosives. Coral reefs are so fragile. Once that live coral dies off, it takes a very long time for the reef to recover, if ever. It's not only looters who damage reefs. Some people don't think. Or they don't know any better. We all just need to take a little more care when we fish and dive."

Still thinking about the treasure, I mused, "Those men found so much stuff. Even without blasting, or digging with a vacuum. Maybe those storms moved the sand around enough to uncover the treasure."

"That's possible, Chad. Very possible," Mr. Panchet said. "As for the treasure being near Sugarloaf, one theory we came up with—years back, when we first worked the site—was that possibly some of the original salvagers from over three hundred years ago, *wreckers*, they were called, recovered some of the treasure from ship wreck sites south of here and then lost it again in the waters up this way. Maybe from another storm. We'll never know for sure how the ancient coins ended up so close to Sugarloaf. It's a pretty good mystery, no? You let me know when you figure it out. Well, you two, I've got something special for you. A little reward." He dug into his pocket with another bristly smile. "Put out your hands, please."

I stuck out my hand. With a solid little *thwap*, a shiny silver coin landed in my hand. A duplicate coin dropped into Georgene's hand.

"It's a piece of eight!" I exclaimed, recognizing the markings from the pictures I'd seen.

Smiling, Georgene bounced the coin lightly in her hand. "It's heavy. Thank you, Mr. Panchet."

"You earned those coins," he said. "Check the markings—you'll see the seal of the Spanish king who commissioned them."

"It's hard to believe this coin was down under the sand and water for over three hundred years," Georgene said quietly as she studied the coin.

Mr. Panchet smiled at her. "It's fascinating, isn't it?"

"Thanks." I rubbed my thumb over the raised marks on the coin. "Wouldn't it be *supreme* if we could to go out on a dive boat, Gene? See how they bring up treasure?" Excited by the feel of the silver, I said it without thinking, but the idea stayed with me as I fought off another huge yawn.

Georgene glanced at Dad and then rolled her eyes at me.

"You know . . ." Mr. Pachet's eyebrows arched into a single dark line. "You're right, Chad, you two should come out on a salvage boat and see what it's really like to dig up buried treasure. It's not nearly as glamorous as people imagine. You'd find out just how much hard slow work it really is."

"Could we?" I looked at Dad. His eyes grew round, but he didn't say anything.

"If your father gives the okay, of course," he added. He paused for a moment, looking at me thoughtfully. "The treasure really is extraordinary, but do you know the best part?"

I was already nodding.

"The hunt. Treasure hunters *believe*," he said. "They keep searching, for as long as it takes. An explorer simply must believe. Remember that, young man. Believe in yourself and never lose hope, no matter what anyone else says."

I stared past him, filing his words away for later as I pictured what it would be like to find treasure buried under the sand at the bottom of the ocean. I half-whispered, "Thanks, Mr. Panchet."

After the men had gone, I hunched low in my chair, busily inspecting my coin. "Dad," I said, then hesitated as I fought off another yawn. "Think we could go with Mr. Panchet? I mean, even after everything that's happened?"

Dad frowned and brushed the hair off my forehead. "You did something very important helping to stop those men, Chad. But no more adventures. My heart can't take it. Right now, you two look like yesterday's bait," he said, with a weary smile. "Time for some sleep."

"Night," I mumbled, too groggy to put up a fight.

Outside my door, Georgene squeezed my arm and leaned down to whisper in my ear, "See you tomorrow, Chad. Thanks."

And with a slow grin I stumbled off to bed.

31

THE NEXT MORNING, I stared down at the shallow water under the dock, waiting for my eyes to adjust to the bright light. Hermit crabs scrambled over the bay's sandy bottom, sea anemones swayed in the current, and schools of glittery glass minnows shot flashes of light as they darted through the gently waving grasses.

I fingered the markings on the silver coin and thought about what Mr. Panchet had told us.

Minutes later, the sound of flip-flops slapping across the boards interrupted the plan shaping in my mind. "You know, Chad, I don't care if we go anywhere else ever again." Georgene sighed happily as she plopped down beside me. "I am just so glad to be back at our dock. It's peaceful here, don't you think?"

Not ready to respond, I kept my eyes on the action under the water.

Leaning in, she grinned up at me. "Hel-*loo?* Anybody there?"

"You know, for once, you're right, Georgene. This is a very good place to be," I agreed with a smile.

"It's nice Mom's finally here," she continued. "I can't believe how calm she's been about everything that's happened. Guess she's just happy we're okay."

I raised my head and stared out at the bright bay. "Hey, Gene? We need to talk to—"

I stopped short, considering the best way to start.

"What's that, Chad?"

"We still have a few days. I think that maybe we should get out on Mr. Panchet's salvage boat before we have to head back home," I said, eyeing her carefully.

The little pilot light sparked in her eyes for just a second, and then it went out just as quickly. "*Chad,*" she said, with a sharp laugh. "Just keep that genius idea to yourself, little brother. I don't want to move off this dock."

"Come on, Gene. A *salvage* boat . . . with real treasure hunting? There's no way I'm going to pass that up," I insisted, grinning confidently. "Know what I mean? If we don't go now, we'll never get out there."

"I am *not* hearing this," said Georgene, her eyes suddenly huge. "I know that look. You're serious!"

"Genie—"

"Nope. Not going to happen." I followed you out there to the reef because you just *had* to find out what those guys were doing, and look at the mess we got into! We made it back here—"

"Exactly," I pronounced.

"...Alive," she finished, jabbing her finger at my chest. "Don't you think we should just park it right here on this peaceful dock until the plane takes off for Philadelphia?"

Getting more excited, I argued, "No, I think we should go find out about salvaging treasure."

She sighed. "Just what are you after this time, Chad?"

With a smile, I replied, "You'll just have to trust me."